From the forgotten queens of sci-fi and horror pulps, to vignettes of Black life in Chicago in the late 1950s, to time-traveling and galaxy-hopping puns, our **Beyond Pulp Reprints** series brings neglected works back into print in editions that are both attractive and affordable.

REQUIEM FOR A SIREN
WOMEN POETS OF THE PULPS

Edited by
Jaclyn Youhana Garver
&
Michael W. Phillips Jr.

Published by From Beyond Press | Chicago, IL
frombeyondpress.com
mike@frombeyondpress
ISBN: 979-8-9875743-8-6
LCCN: 2024948926

Contents

Traffic not with ghosts
Lest if you do
You find their world
More real than earth to you.

Dorothy Quick, "Unsought Advice"
Weird Tales, May 1937

Introduction
A Place for Wild Women

Dorothy Quick was one of almost three hundred women who published fiction and poetry in sci-fi and horror pulp magazines before 1960.

Have you heard of her?

Her name may be familiar to the genre's uber fans, but it's never mentioned alongside the likes of the Big Three—H.P. Lovecraft, Clark Ashton Smith, and Robert E. Howard—and it should be. Between 1932 and 1954, Quick published fifteen stories in *Weird Tales*, placing her just outside the top twenty most prolific fiction writers in that storied magazine. She also published twenty-four poems, good for fourth-most, tied with Leah Bodine Drake—which is another name you may be unfamiliar with. Those first three spots went to the aforementioned Big Three.

This is a book of poetry published by women in pulp magazines between 1919 and 1953. "Pulp" is a catch-all term used to describe genre fiction magazines in the first half of the twentieth century, named after the cheap wood-pulp paper they were printed on.

While the early days of pulp were dominated by men, women made a sizable and important contribution to the genre, which might come as a surprise. It's a common misconception that horror and sci-fi was unwelcoming to women in its early days, that women needed to hide behind initials or pseudonyms to get noticed by the sexist editors of the day. But women were essential to the success of pulp horror and sci-fi. Women read it. Wrote it. Edited it. Joined horror fan clubs. Wrote fan mail to horror magazines. As award-winning horror writer Paula D. Ashe told us, "Horror has always been a place for wild women."

Just look at *Weird Tales*, the flagship magazine of the pulp horror flotilla. According to University of Pittsburgh political history professor Eric Leif Davin, author of *Partners in Wonder: Women and the Birth of Science Fiction, 1926-1965*, *Weird Tales* always published women.

Dorothy McIlwraith edited it for almost half its original run. Its most famous cover artist was Margaret Brundage, known as "the First Lady of pulp magazine illustration" (she's responsible for that gorgeous siren on the cover of this book). *Weird Tales*'s readership was over a quarter women, and its fan club was between a quarter and a third women. Seventeen percent of its fiction authors and 40 percent of its poets were women.

So much for the idea that weird fiction was a boy's club.

And those statistics cover just the gender-identifiable women. There's no way to know how many of the authors who used initials were women, or how many women published under masculine pseudonyms or masculine-sounding names, like Gerald Chan Sieg, included in this collection.

Forgotten for decades, the fiction-writing women of the pulps have finally begun to get their due in collections like Valancourt's *Women of Weird Tales*, the British Library's *Queens of the Abyss*, and our own *Fettered and Other Tales of Terror* by Greye La Spina. But classic horror and sci-fi poetry generally receives short shrift if it's not by Lovecraft, Smith, or Howard.

This book is a step in correcting that omission.

While we researched the lives of the women who wrote these poems, we came across an article in the *Boston Globe* about Brooke Byrne, a librarian who was likely the same Brooke Byrne who wrote the poem "Sic Transit Gloria," included in this book. As part of her job, Byrne repaired irreplaceable books. She told the *Globe* reporter, "To save a book from physical destruction—a book which is out of print, which exists by sheer chance against the odds of time—that, to me, is a challenge."

Existing "by sheer chance against the odds of time" . . . we can't think of a better way to describe the poems in this book. They are written in an outmoded style and a disreputable genre, they were printed on cheap paper, and then they were forgotten, their copyrights long lapsed. But thanks to the efforts of collectors and archivists—especially those at the Internet Archive, where we found almost everything in this book—they're still here and ready for reappraisal.

Poetry, like any other art, like anything else in popular culture, follows trends. The oldest poems are heroic epics, the very earliest dating to around 3,000 BCE. The *Epic of Gilgamesh* originated in ancient Mesopotamia and told the tale of the king of Uruk's quest for immortality after the gods killed his companion Enkidu.

Which is a far cry from religious hymns. Which are far cries from Shakespearean sonnets, with their rigid meter and rhyme scheme, often requiring multiple reads to follow. Which are far cries from today's poetry royalty, like U.S. poet laureate Ada Limón and her accessible, stirring free verse.

By comparison to all that, the poetry in these pages might be seen as simplistic. Much of it follows such a set cadence that it's sing-songy; some wouldn't look out of place in the pages of a children's book. There's the kind of end rhyme that approaches obviousness; to illustrate, Jaclyn scrolled quickly through this Google Document we're writing in and stopped at random. The first three stanzas in the poem she landed on ended with deep/sleep, flame/name, grace/face.

Eric Williams, editor of *Night Fears: Weird Tales in Translation*, told us that this stylistic choice comes from two sources: (1) a desire to emulate Edgar Allan Poe and (2) anti-modernism. The Poe connection is obvious if you're familiar with his poetry: ballad forms, line repetition, simple rhyme schemes, an obsession with lost loves and inevitable death and passion that persists beyond the grave. Not to imply that the women in this collection aped Poe, but they were certainly familiar with his work, and Poe-worship seems to have been the ethos of the *Weird Tales* poetry oeuvre.

As for anti-modernism, that's more complicated. In the early 20th century, artists, writers, poets, and musicians started abandoning earlier forms—strict meter for poems, realism in paintings, etc.—in favor of abstraction, subjectivity, and experimentation. The modernist nuclear bomb in poetry, T.S. Eliot's *The Waste Land*, may be the most famous example. The piece is so influential that H.P. Lovecraft wrote his own epic "modernist" poem, "Waste Paper: A Poem of Profound Insignificance," which mocked Eliot's. (Although, like the best satire, "Waste Paper" shows a deep understanding of its target and is a pretty good modernist poem in its own right.) Lovecraft wasn't alone in his stance: one of our poets, Lilith Lorraine, started a foundation dedicated to fighting against modernism in the arts.

Modernism changed poetry, and it changed people's relationship to poetry. Once, poems were popular—so popular that Yetza Gillespie, one of our poets, was able to sell 100 poems a year. Part of that popularity is due to the fact that newspapers and magazines almost always included poetry, allowing readers to sit with, for example, a rhyming poem about nature or marriage over their morning coffee. When poetry stopped rhyming, it became a niche genre, and periodicals stopped printing it—so people stopped reading poetry as often.

But those old-fashioned techniques of rhyme and meter belie the pain and mystery in the verse. The poem whose rhyme scheme we laid out a few paragraphs ago is titled "The Suicide's Awakening," and the speaker appears to be stuck in a limbo of her own doing, confused and frightened. These poems may sound like nursery rhymes, but they're certainly not intended for children.

Topically, to follow the trends in horror is to catalog the fears of a society. In *Horror's Greatest*, a Shudder documentary series that focuses on a variety of horror sub-genres, film scholar Todd Kushigemachi said this about *Godzilla*, or *Gojira* in Japanese, in an episode devoted to giant monsters: "*Gojira* might be one of the quintessential examples of using horror or sort of fantastic elements to deal with trauma in a way that maybe if you dealt with it more directly, then people wouldn't just want to talk about it. This is nine years after the end of World War II. I think about the atomic bombings of Nagasaki and Hiroshima."

What do these poems say about the societal fears of the women who wrote them? We divided the collection by theme and saw immediately that there were many haunted houses. There were many monsters. There was much about lost love and about women behaving wildly. The vast majority of the poems were published in the 1930s, '40s, and '50s. Yes, more women entered the workforce after the 1929 stock market crash, though most of the positions available to women were so-called women's work—domestic service, teaching, clerical work—that weren't hit by the Great Depression like coal mining and manufacturing, which mostly employed men. The 1930s saw a 22 percent decline in marriage, so more women were supporting themselves.[1]

By 1945, one in four married women was working outside the home. Still, by 1950, women made up less than 30 percent of the workforce.[2]

Focusing on ghosts and ghouls and monsters at home? On lost loves? On behaving "badly," or in a way that society deemed inappropriate? It sure does seem to fit neatly into the vibes of the era.

So light some candles and turn off the lights. Pull a comfortable chair up to the fire. Read some of these poems aloud—but not too loudly, or you might summon something with too many eyes, or no eyes at all. You might summon something from beneath the waves or beyond the stars. And keep Dorothy Quick's "Unsought Advice" in mind, lest you find the worlds created by the women in this book *More real than earth to you.*

A Note on Sources

We followed these steps to find the poems included in this collection:

1. Original sources: We drew these poems from professional horror and sci-fi magazines published between the 1919 debut of *The Thrill Book*—the first magazine to prioritize speculative fiction—and the end of the original run of *Weird Tales* in 1954. Other sources included *Amazing Stories, Famous Fantastic Mysteries, Fantasy Book,* and *Super Science Stories.* There were other speculative fiction magazines around during this period, but they didn't publish poetry or any poetry by women.

When we say "professional horror and sci-fi magazines," we mean magazines that paid their authors and were printed and distributed commercially, the same as any popular magazine. You could go to a newsstand (RIP) and find these magazines alongside *Cosmopolitan* and *Ranch Romances* (a real thing) (RIP).

We excluded poems published in so-called fanzines, which were magazines or newsletters with varying levels of professionalism. They were often typed on a typewriter, mimeographed, and mailed to a small group of people. The importance of fanzines to the growth of speculative fiction, and especially speculative poetry, cannot be overstated (check out our bio of Lilith Lorraine in the first chapter), but to welcome those sources into this book would have given us an impossible amount of material to sift through.

Every rule has an exception, and ours was *Dark of the Moon: Poems of Fantasy and the Macabre,* a book edited by August Derleth and published by his Arkham House in 1947. Derleth was a *Weird Tales* stalwart, a friend to many of the writers who published there, and a tireless champion of weird fiction and poetry. His collection contained poems by many of the women who appeared in *Weird Tales* and was published during its original run, so we included work from it.

2. Poems considered: To come up with our list of possible poems to include from those sources, we consulted tables of contents available at the Internet Speculative Fiction Database, an exhaustive online catalog of just about every horror and science fiction thing ever published.

We limited our pool to poets who were identifiably women: those with feminine names or who were otherwise known to identify as women. Although many poets who went by their first initials and last name were undoubtedly women, we couldn't know for sure, so we excluded them. Also, we acknowledge that some of our "women" might have been men writing under a pseudonym.

3. Poems selected: Our final list of possibilities contained 213 poems, which we narrowed down to 102 through the magic of color coding: Green meant "I love this, let's include it." Yellow meant, "Eh, I can take it or leave it." Red meant, "Oh, hell, no." To make the cut, the poem had to receive two green checks of approval, or one green and one yellow. We each went to bat for a couple poems the other redded out. Sometimes, we even won.

We looked for poems that spoke to us, which is an admittedly subjective criteria. Poetry is deeply personal for a reader. A poem that made Jaclyn's pulse race like a genuine jump scare might have made Mike yawn like a slow burn with a boring reveal. And vice versa.

Did we probably miss some? Of course. We hope you'll forgive us the oversight.

And then we hope this collection prompts you to go find more.

A Note on Organization

We divided the 102 poems into ten themed chapters. Each chapter has an introductory essay that either puts the poems in their historical and social context or talks about our personal relationships with the work. We singled out one author from each chapter for a longer biographical profile, with shorter bios in the back. These ten poets with longer bios aren't necessarily the most famous or prolific authors; instead, they're those whose lives we found fascinating or who helped illustrate the process of putting this book together.

Jaclyn Youhana Garver & Michael W. Phillips Jr.

Notes

1. Jessica Pearce Rotondi, "Underpaid, But Employed: How the Great Depression Affected Working Women," history.com/news/working-women-great-depression
2. San Diego Air and Space Museum, "Women Factory Workers of WWII: Going to War," sandiegoairandspace.org/exhibits/online-exhibit-page/women-factory-workers-of-world-war-ii-overview; Val Fox, "1940s: Women Join the WWII Arms Race," www.bentley.edu/news/photo-journey-through-50-years-women-work

The Jealous Sea Calls Back Its Own
Aquatic Horror Poems

The two most famous horror poets in history both lived at the edge of the sea: Edgar Allan Poe in Boston and Baltimore and H.P. Lovecraft in Providence, Rhode Island. So it's not surprising to find so many verses of oceanic terror among our offerings—Poe's shadow hangs over nearly everything in *Weird Tales*, and Lovecraft influenced much of the horror poetry and prose that came after him.

Poe returned to the sea for inspiration again and again, such as in his early work "The City in the Sea" and more famously "Annabel Lee," with its haunting refrain *In this kingdom by the sea*. Lovecraft saw the ocean as a vast, terrifying unknown, beneath which dwelled elder gods, including Cthulhu himself, who awaits in deathlike sleep in the sunken city of R'lyeh. Even earlier than Poe, the sea was fodder for frightful lyric poems, most famously Samuel Taylor Coleridge's *The Rime of the Ancient Mariner*, with its *spirits from the land of mist and snow* and its *slimy things (that) did crawl with legs / Upon the slimy sea.*

So I laughed out loud when I learned that this book's most prominent versifier of terrifying aquatic settings, Leah Bodine Drake, lived her entire life inland. She was born in Kentucky and also lived in Indiana and West Virginia. So much for "write what you know."

What she did know was how to make you afraid of things, damp or not, in rhyming couplets: the kicker at the end of "Revenant" is one of my favorite moments in this book. The narrator of that poem is joined in this chapter by ghost ships, half-human/half-seal hybrids who don't fit in on land or under the waves, and heartbroken women scanning the tides for their lost lovers who will never return—or worse, the ones even death can't keep away.

Happy sailing.

Michael W. Phillips Jr.

Revenant
Leah Bodine Drake

Now up the shore
    The ripples slide;
The full moon pulls
    The haunted tide,

The lamp leaps up
    In the cottage pane,
And I am up
    From the depths again.

Wild with sorrow,
    My spirit beats
Up-wind to where
    The sea-sand meets

The darkened soil
    Of furrowed land,
Where the little church
    And the gravestones stand.

I know one headstone
    White and cold,
Whose carven lie
    States through the mold:

"God rest our darling
    Drowned at sea."
The calm earth-grave
    Holds none of me!

Even my spirit
    Cannot stay
Where the graveyard grasses
    Bend like spray.

For the jealous sea
      Calls back its own
Through the warm earth calls
      To the sea-held bone,

And there is no rest
      In the old, kind ground
For the bones unblest
      Of one self-drowned!

Weird Tales, March 1951

Long Watch
Dorothy Quick

Daughter, the tide is running low.
Is it the wind that is sobbing so?
What of the rocks and the undertow
And those long gray miles where the gray ships go?

Daughter, the tide will turn at last.
Is it your heart that beats so fast?
Whose ensign flies from the tilted mast?
In what strange port was the anchor cast?

Daughter, many a long night through
I've tried forgetting, the same as you.
Did you trim the lamp, as I told you to?
The sea's a lover. It's true, it's true!

The tide turns back and the storms abate,
Daughter, remember soon or late
And ships come home with their precious freight,
No matter if women watch and wait!

Weird Tales, July 1946

Fog
Cristel Hastings

Long ghostly fingers of the dripping mist
Grope silently among the ships that list
To port and starboard along lonely piers
Whose boards know sodden taste of salty tears.

From bow to keel there is the constant sound
Of water—water—water all around—
Of tides that ebb and flow the long night through,
And clinging veils of mist that hide the blue.

A tearful lot is that of ships men tie
'Longside some crumbling wharf where shadows lie
Waiting for measured tread on decks that seem
The pathway of old mariners who dream.

Somewhere in sand lots, looking out to sea
And counting ships in clouds that quickly flee
A gale—ah, ships that wait beside old piers;
You have the wind—the ancient tides of years

And fog that mourns the watered graves of them
While winds all chant a sobbing requiem
In mourning as a grayish phantom hull
Drifts by, her only passenger a gull.

Weird Tales, April 1932

The House by the Sea

Frances Elliott

A graying image sedged with rutted grass,
    With curtained eyes it faces the slow hours
    As immobile as dustless waxen flowers
Embalmed beneath dim sterile globes of glass.
Its darkened contours blot from out its sight
    The flashing suns that seek the destiny
    Of twilight seas; and crystal mystery
Of quivering waves that leap into the night.

The roses blow untended by the wall,
    The hyacinth spills perfume to the spring;
    Along the dunes the lilting sea winds sing
As masted ships ride by to ports of call.
And men forget the secret of the dream
That fires its tapers with a pallid gleam.

Weird Tales, August 1933

The Mermaid
Leah Bodine Drake

Flashing through facets of her glassy world
The many-chambered sea, cold mermaid rises,
For a lean shadow now obliquely moves
Across her rippled roof.

Up, up, up from her hollowed water-land,
Up convoluted stairways of her restless house
The mermaid mounts, shaking her dangerous hair,
And see! she spreads before the vessel's bow
Her gold-green locks and scarlet seaweed crown,
Her pearly-pale half-body of a girl
Cupped in its husk of opalescent scale.

Who flushes red, and leaps, and in her arms
Sinks with a bubbled cry of fear and joy,
But he the youngest of the gaping crew?
O call in vain to your lost brother, fling the net,
Tough powerless fishers straining desperate-eyed
Against the dripping side!
Then bid the women on the hungry shore
Raise the wild keen and wring their empty hands!

Far out the mermaid, tired of her play,
Lets her chill toy drift weathercock, supine,
In hammocks of the swinging tides, while she
Flicks a bright fin and darts to comb her curls
Among rough water-rocks off Brittany.

Weird Tales, November 1952

The Sea King's Daughter
Dorothy Quick

The Sea King's Daughter rides the waves.
The Sea King's Daughter who is so fair,
That men go gladly to their graves
If they can but touch her shining hair.

The Sea King's Daughter's hair is green,
Green as the glint of an emerald eye.
The cold sea water reflects its sheen
And calls to the men who are sailing by.

The Sea King's Daughter's lure is strong
So the men reach out for her and death.
She knows the right, she knows the wrong
But her warning call is a lost breath.

The Sea King's Daughter has no home,
She weeps for love she can never know
Till her tears churn up in an angry foam
As she beats the surf wild breezes blow.

The Sea King's Daughter, always alone.
Alone with the Sun, the wind and air,
With never a roof to call her own
Or a place to hide her shining hair.

Weird Tales, January 1950

The Titan's Goblet

Lilith Lorraine

Drink from the Titan's goblet,
You who would ravish space,
Drink till you reel and stagger,
Drink till your pulses race

With the wine that was brewed of moon-blood
At the edge of chaos-brink
For all that the gods have left you
Is the chalice—and the drink.

Touch your lips to the chalice
Before you quaff your fill,
Savor the mellow cities
Crunch their bones if you will.

Taste of the tall ships floating,
They—they are only foam,
But the wild, sharp tang of waters
And the bells in a sunken dome

Lure you to drink still deeper
Till your mind is the Titan's mind,
Till you whirl through the stars unshackled
By the earth you leave behind.

Drink till the moons melt madly
Under your kiss like snow,
But never ask in your wine-cups
Where did the Titans go?

Super Science Stories, September 1950

The Seal-Woman's Daughter
Leah Bodine Drake

I am half of the land
    And half of the water,
For my dam was a seal
    And I am her daughter.

I am sib to the land
    And kin to the sea,
For my dam was a seal
    But a king sired me.

My father has built me
    A tapestry'd bower
Where twelve duke's daughters
    Serve hour by hour.

Heroes and princes
    Come wooing me,
But there is not one
    Who smells of the sea!

My old nurse tells me
    That I must beware
When I walk on the shore
    With my unbound hair.

For out of the cold sea
    A lover may rise,
Dark, sleek and furry,
    With seal-brown eyes.

So I walk on the sands
    When the gray winds blow,
Afraid of the waves
    And what's below.

I sit with my maidens
	And weave at my loom,
And my flesh rebels
	At the fire-warm room.

For I'm not all beast
	And I'm not quite human,
Who has eyes of a seal
	In the face of a woman.

And where can I rest,
	A brown seal's daughter,
Who hates the land
	And fears the water?

Weird Tales, January 1947

The River
Dorothy Quick

Down by the river early, early
    Under the lowering unclear light,
The rising sun is surly, surly,
    And nothing's distinct or over-bright,
And then the river dances, dances
    With water the moon has driven mad
And willow trees send glances, glances
    That are unearthly, cold and sad.

Down by the river slowly, slowly
    The sun will rise, the dancing cease,
The willow trees bend lowly, lowly
    As the river once again knows peace.

Weird Tales, September 1948

Sea-Shell
Leah Bodine Drake

Stranded upon the sand
Here is a twisted shell:
Lift it within your hand,
Press it against your ear;
Listen! . . . and you will hear
Echo of deep-sea bell
Ringing in belfry beneath the brine,
Where mermaidens, scaled with tourmaline,
Toll a dolorous knell.
'Tis the voice of a city beneath the sea!
Gold-eyed fishes stare endlessly
At turrets and ramparts of porphyry
Drowned in a gold-green well.

Who built that city forlorn?
What was its perilous fame
That tymbal and gong and horn
Blared from the torch-lit wall?
When did its doom befall?
What was the reason it came
Crashing down over palace and keep
A sea that rose like a mountain steep,
Quenching the living flame?
Hark! . . . do the sea-shell's echoes tell
The name of that city before she fell?
Ah, no, I can hear its cry, its bell,
But never its fabulous name!

Weird Tales, September 1943

The Specter's Tale
Yetza Gillespie

An awesome thing happened
In a sea coast town,
When the herrings schooled
And the moon hung down.

The men were reaping silver
They never had sown
With a net for a sickle
In a field never mown.

Womenfolk of prudence
Were thankful for a lock,
Knitting by the hearth-fire,
Deaf to a knock.

But, oh! the wind was calling
Through the crack in the door,
And one less was minded
Of the curved white shore.

She never saw the shadow,
Or the boat in the cove,
Till she was treasure added
To the pirates' trove.

A man must be heedful
To handle a boat—
And knives are keen and thirsty
For a Turkoman's throat.

A lass might win the shingle
Who knew the tides well,
And a dead body rolling
With its soul in hell

Is heart-freezing company.
He died with a curse.
Those waiting on shipboard
Were living, but worse.

Water-fear is weaker
Than the pull of the land;
Ravishers less certain
Than a lover's own hand.

Some queer woeful catches
Are lifted at last
From snares under water
That rock held fast.

When a seine is lifted
Oh, it is a bitter thing
To see a gold-haired lassie,
And your own pledged ring!

In time he lost the heart-break
Of the limpet on her cheek;
But his grey hairs remembered
How her hands trailed weak

Fingers in the meshes
Of a herring-net
What her breastbone cradled
He never could forget.

Long past and gone like driftwood
This sorrow of the sea.
Oh, very well I know it—
For it happened to me.

Dark of the Moon anthology

Siren Spotlight on Leah Bodine Drake

"There is an idea popular with non-poets that every man is a poet in his youth, and in his youth only. After that, his poetic arteries harden and he gives up verses and devotes himself to prose."

So Leah Bodine Drake (1904–1964) began a June 1957 review of new work in *The Atlantic* magazine. Drake—a poet, editor, reviewer, and, for a short time in Fort Worth, Texas, dancer—remained steeped in poetry through much of her life, publishing over the course of twenty years. *Weird Tales* printed nearly two dozen of her poems, making her the magazine's second most-published female poet, after Dorothy Quick.

Drake's work found commercial success, too, also appearing in *The Atlantic* and being selected for publication out of an average of 1,500 poems received a month, according to the magazine in 1955.

"(Poetry submissions) come as frequently from men as from women, and are evidence of an interest in poetry which never slackens," according to the magazine, underlining yet again the vibrancy and heft of poetry available by women during that time period. (The writeup, it's worth noting, does not mention if the magazine published an equal number of women and men—just that it received poems written by as many women as men.)

Drake lived in many parts of the country throughout her life: She was born in Kansas, spent time during childhood in the deep south, lived in Texas, spent 15 years in Indiana, and died in West Virginia. Her years in the south inspired much of the grim, weird, pulpy poetry she would one day write: "(H)er choice of the macabre in poetry comes naturally, for her earliest memories include the tremendous silences of the Navajo country, the woods and swamps of the deep South," as well as stories of "ha'nts" told by a member of the household, according to the jacket material of Drake's *A Hornbook for Witches*, which includes poetry readers can find on YouTube, as read by Vincent Price.

Jaclyn Youhana Garver

Silence Older than the Cypresses
Arboreal Horror Poems

The deepest darkness I've ever experienced was in the woods. I was a shy, perpetually anxious, bookish kid, and my father took the family to hell: camping in the Manistee National Forest. Not at a campground—in a clearing out in the woods, miles from the nearest paved road. Walking through the forest, he pointed out all the things that could kill or maim us: Don't touch this plant. Don't eat these mushrooms. Don't drink this water. There was no electricity, no running water. No moon.

Fueled by a *Friday the 13th* marathon at my older sister's birthday party, my imagination ran wild. The woods were full of furtive sounds that I just knew were made by masked killers armed with machetes. Possibly bears. Masked bears with machetes.

I woke in the wee hours and had to pee. The thought of leaving the flimsy safety of the tent and entering that absolute darkness paralyzed me, so I urinated in the corner, soaking my sleeping bag. But it was worth the dampness and my father's anger to avoid going out in that terrible, endless forest night.

Now, I go camping every year, but it's at the kind of campground that has showers, electricity, and a little store where you can buy s'mores fixings and batteries for your flashlights.

That camping trip popped into my head as I was reading (and adoring) this chapter's poems, all of which deal at least in part with the wilderness. They sum up the attraction of horror so succinctly: The forest at night is a dreadful place, and the prospect of tasting a bit of that dread from the safety of your couch is irresistible. It's also fun as hell. As Grace Stillman puts it in "The Woods of Averoigne," inspired by the setting for many of Clark Ashton Smith's stories:

Knowing it well, my feet still grope
    Nearer this force malign, withdrawn

In dread, against my will I creep
    Deep in the woods of Averoigne.

You can't resist going into the forest. You can't resist going back.

The woods here are full of what M. Ludington Cain calls *solitude that chills the heart / As some cold, creeping death.* Be careful where you step, because you might find something deadly along the way—or maybe that's what you're looking for? Page Cooper's "The Curse" and Marion Doyle's "In a Dark Wood" could serve as homicidal shopping lists: Cooper warns *Touch no yarrow and taste no scud / Of foxglove wine from a ghost girl's cup*; and Doyle's narrator *had seen the pearly cup on the floor / Of the forest, under a monstrous tree, / And she knew what the end was meant to be.*

It may be that these haunted woods are most dangerous for people looking for a thrill. What if you can't get enough? As Dorothy Quick tells us in "Forest God":

Still it's worth the risking
    Loneliness and pain,
To have the hope to cherish
    Pan might come again.

Just remember to bring a flashlight.

Michael W. Phillips Jr.

In Planders' Wood
M. Ludington Cain

In Planders' wood as sunset fades
The shadows quickly fill
The deep ravines, the mossy glades—
Even the owls are still . . .

No children come to Planders' wood
To gather flowers by day;
If there is breeze the solitude
Soon frightens it away—

A solitude that chills the heart
As some cold, creeping death,
A solitude that tears apart
The fabric of the breath . . .

I have not walked in Planders' wood
For twenty years or more,
There is no smallest likelihood
I shall another score.

My footsteps will not venture where
A mound is . . . overgrown.
I could not go with others there . . .
I dare not go alone. . . .

Famous Fantastic Mysteries, October 1950

The Curse
Page Cooper

When the moon is dark as a black bat's throat,
The stars are hidden, the night is dim,
The dead air shivers at grunt of stoat
Rootling the leaves where grave stones glim.

Beware of the herbs with their leaves stemmed up
Touch no yarrow and taste no scud
Of foxglove wine from a ghost girl's cup,
Drink no philtre of lapwing's blood.

Make no mock of the black jay's mate
Nor the witless grief of the mourning dove,
Or you'll die of loving what you should hate,
Cursed with hating what you should love.

Weird Tales, January 1942

The Others Said

Katherine Simons

The others said: "It's the autumn leaves."
    But I heard its feet in the guttered eaves
On moonless nights when the stars were blurred
    And the wind in the palm trees sobbed and slurred.

The others said: "It's a bird that flies."
    But I watched for green in the evening skies
A harbinger; and the others slept
    While it mewed on the shingled roof and crept.

The others said: "You have fallen ill
    "From the noonday heat or the midnight chill."
But I saw its eyes and I felt its breath
    And I know its chill is the cold of death.

Weird Tales, September 1947

The Ultimate Word
Marion Doyle

Always there has been something not quite said;
    Something that sunlight sifted down through leaves,
Starlight on water, and the echoes shed
    From slow rain's whisper in deserted eaves
Tried to interpret in my slower tongue. . . .

Once, long ago—oh, very long ago—
    Before the world was old, and I was young,
I *almost* grasped the Word in flakes of snow,
    In fireflies like golden spangles flung
Across a dancer's twilight-colored hair,
    In spider-webs miraculously strung
With a gnome-king's ransom in the morning air. . . .

But that was long ago—oh, so long ago—
    Before the world was old, and I was young.

Weird Tales, October 1933

Swamp Symphony
Cristel Hastings

What do they croak about all the night long—
The frogs in the swamp—is it sorrow or song?
Who wields the baton as it marks the slow time
For the shadowy phantoms who dwell in the slime?

Do wraiths haunt the marshland and dance to the tunes
The wind in the reeds plays among the gray dunes?
And why does the moon hide her face in the fog
As shapes wrapped in darkness glide over the bog?

What is the sighing and moaning that sounds
Like thin vapor whispers from grass-matted mounds?
What stirs the glazed surface of waters long dead—
And what is that Thing without eyes in its head?

The clammy winds whimper and wail in their fright,
Making a dirge of the low sounds of night;
Loneliness grasps the thin throat of a ghost
And shakes till it rattles the bones of its host.

All through the shrill night the frogs drum their lay
And pipe the slow measures for shapes, dim and gray,
Until reckless dawn sends an arrow of light
To still the mad opera that haunted the night.

Weird Tales, March 1930

In a Dark Wood
Marion Doyle

She came to a wood of twisted trees
Where claw-like roots clutched at her knees;
    A bracken thrust its threatening frond
    Into her heart; a stagnant pond
Spread treacherous iris to ensnare
Bewildered feet in a sinking lair;
    Flung from its farthest edge, a briar
    Seared her eyes like living fire,
Blinding her utterly; but before,
She had seen the pearly cup on the floor
    Of the forest, under a monstrous tree,
    And she knew what the end was meant to be:

No going back the way she came
(No more of quicksand, sword and flame)
    To crystal springs.
She knelt by the dank
Destroying Angel's cup—and drank.

Weird Tales, May 1939

Tree Woman
Dorothy Quick

Deep in the fastness of a Druid wood
She saw no path between the somber trees;
Leaf-mold and moss were dank, and where she stood
Silence was older than the cypresses.
There crept along her veins a chilly flow
Of something not of flesh; her fingers curled
On emptiness. Ten thousand years ago
This might have been the dawn-dusk of the world!

Strange how her feet were rooted there; she heard
Her lips moan like the wind; her arms, uptossed,
Were long and supple, and a dark-winged bird
Perched on her shoulder. Beautiful and lost,
She felt upon her brow, once white and fair,
A crown of leaves that rustled softly there!

Weird Tales, March 1946

The Piper of the Pines
Marjorie Holmes

Oh slim, shrill piper
    Playing to the pines,
Drunk on autumn liquor,
    Drunk on purple wines,
Mimicking the wind-song
    On your magic flute,
In your forest medley
    Hear the owls hoot,
Hear the wolf-pups whimper,
    And the coyotes cry,
In the awful answer
    Hear the eagle die!

Weird, gay piper,
    In the garb of green,
Grinning, grimly grinning,
Lank and loose and lean. . . .
Oh piper, fling your pipes away,
    Piper, hush! No longer play,
For I loathe your music shrill—
    Maddened piper on the hill.

See him peek beneath the trees,
    See him hop about, and then
Hear him, laughing in the breeze,
    Lift his pipes and play again!

Weird Tales, April-May 1931

Forest God
Dorothy Quick

Keep out of the forest
    Harken to advice,
For those whom Pan caresses
    Never see him twice.

Those who know Pan's touches
    And those who feel Pan's kiss
Know that there is nothing
    Ever to equal this.

Those who hear Pan's music
    And look into Pan's eyes,
Will always hear his laughter,
    Will always be too wise.

Still it's worth the risking
    Loneliness and pain,
To have the hope to cherish
    Pan might come again.

Weird Tales, November 1949

The Woods of Averoigne
(Inspired by Clark Ashton Smith's stories)
Grace Stillman

Deep in the woods of Averoigne,
    Goblin and satyr, loup-garou,
Devil and vampire hold their feasts:
    Forces of wizardry imbue
Even the foliage of the oak;
    Beeches and pines in drear decay
Uplift their bony branches wan
    Under a sky of corpse-like gray.
Evil is there in Averoigne:
    Evil I should not see at all;
Evil whose very presence seems
    Holding me in a curious thrall:
Knowing it well, my feet still grope
    Nearer this force malign, withdrawn;
In dread, against my will I creep
    Deep in the woods of Averoigne.

Weird Tales, June 1934

Siren Spotlight on M. Ludington Cain

Maude Ludington Cain (1886–1965) was a widely published, prize-winning poet and a member of American Pen Women and American Poetry League, according to the Marshall County Historical Society in Iowa, where she lived most of her life.

Her life story is the stuff of *Weird Tales* fiction: Orphaned at a young age, Cain was adopted by Rev. Isaac Newton Cain and his wife, Dr. Mary Archer, who were missionaries to Africa from the United Brethren of the Church of Christ. The two were killed in a massacre in Sierra Leone in 1898; thankfully Cain was at boarding school in the United States at the time. She studied at a music conservatory and then at Whitewater State Teachers College in Wisconsin.

She enjoyed entering slogan contests, telling the *Des Moines Tribune* that "it sharpens your wits." She was good, too: In 1923, she won a third prize of $1000 in a contest sponsored by the National Lumber Manufacturers' Association to find a slogan for wood. (Her entry, "Wood: Use It; Nature Renews It" lost to "Certified by Centuries of Service." She was robbed.) She also wrote the dedication on the Marshalltown Cemetery's World War II memorial.

She published three poems in *Weird Tales* competitor magazines, as well as many other poems in mainstream outlets including *American Mercury*, *New York Herald Tribune*, and *Chicago Tribune*. "Don't let anyone think there's much financial return for writing poetry," she said in 1955. "You're lucky if you can get your postage back."

Michael W. Phillips Jr.

A New Star Brightly Blinking
Poems of Science, Space, and the Future

As we mentioned in the introduction, most of the poems in this book appeared in *Weird Tales*, because no other professional speculative fiction magazine made poetry such a central part of its offerings. But the poetry in *WT* was mostly horror, not science fiction.

Weird Tales also wasn't generally very funny. Sure, there's black comedy among its fiction offerings, but most of the poems were dead serious. (I was going to say "Try to imagine H.P. Lovecraft cracking a joke." He's probably not very high on your internal list of the funniest horror writers around. Look at the man's face—he may not be on your list at all. But he had a hell of a sense of humor, and it occasionally came out in verse, as we mentioned in the introduction. Anyway, back to the ladies, of which Lovecraft was not one.)

By casting a wider net, we were able to include sci-fi poems by women in *Amazing Stories*, *Super Science Stories*, and especially *Fantasy Book*, whose poetry column was edited by Lilith Lorraine.

Along the way, we discovered that sci-fi comedy poetry was very much a thing—a thing, we trust you will agree, that the world needs more of. So this section—intended to collect poems about science, science fiction, space, and the future—also ended up being funny. Julia Boynton Green emerges as the prima science fiction comedienne of the pulps. In "Evolution," she remarks, *Often when strolling idly out of doors / The joy of upright carriage thrills me through.* Who among us has not felt the same thrill? And the narrator of "Radio Revelations" tunes into a galactic gossip network, including this gem about Orion's indecency: *Or is it that he loves to pose / In just his belt and bludgeon?*

But fear not! We have not abandoned our quest to bring you rhyming couplets of doom and damnation. Some of this stuff is dark and cold as nuclear winter, especially poems from the post-World War II, post-atomic bomb years. Rita Barr gives us a "Lost Earth" where mankind

Was impelled by a demon-curse
To pluck the fruit of the atom-tree
And shatter the universe.

Meanwhile, Lilith Lorraine writes of a "Mutation" born after a nuclear war who curses the forebears who cursed him: *(he) clenched six fists beneath the sky, / Cursed with two mouths and glared with one red eye.* Lucrezia Reynard warns about the damage that rapacious capitalism is doing to the earth, envisioning a future where all that's left is *a vast steel graveyard / as a final monument / to free enterprise.* (And for those keeping count, Reynard's "Chief Engineer" is one of only two poems in this book that don't rhyme.)

And we close this section with Enola Chamberlain's poem about a future Earth that's such a black hole of negativity that passing ships avoid it: *Feel how her hate waves keep our space ship swaying, / How anger buffets us from off our course.*

We're ready for takeoff. Buckle your seatbelts—it's going to be a bumpy ride.

Michael W. Phillips Jr.

The Star-Gazer Climbs
Hazel Burden

Bind my hair upon my head,
    Fasten up my shoon;
Tonight I travel far and far
    Toward the golden moon.

Tonight I tread the Milky Way
    On prism paths of stars,
And journey through the Pleiades,
    And set my foot on Mars.

I shall go far on eager feet,
    Straight through the Milky Way,
And scatter star-dust all around
    On those who bid me stay.

But I'll return to earth again,
    Though on reluctant feet,
To walk on patterned paths once more
    In raiment straight and neat.

And you will never know, my dear,
    And you will never care
To climb the heights that I have climbed,
    Or do the deeds I'd dare.

Weird Tales, February 1934

Radio Revelations
Julia Boynton Green

Before John's new receiving set
I listened, half-expecting
The music of the spheres to get,
Some stellar fugue or canzonet,
Man's chatter intersecting.
Instead, from empyrean heights
Celestial gossip drifted;
The greater and the lesser lights
It seems have frolics, feuds, and fights,
Even as the less uplifted.

"It's scandalous how Orion goes,"
Quoth Vega in high dudgeon,
"Can't he afford some pants and hose?
Or is it that he loves to pose
In just his belt and bludgeon?"
Then Vesta scolded, "Listen, pray!
Those wild beasts—where's their cager?
As I went down the Milky Way
To get my Pasteurized Grade A
He *bit* me—Ursa Major!

Of course, surprised, I had no show—
I whacked him with my slipper,
But Aries, Serpens, Scorpio
And Taurus joined the scrap and so
I brandished the Big Dipper.
Then pranced up Sagittarius
And shot them! How I kissed him!
We two then harnessed Pegasus
To Charles's Wain—absurd old bus—
And ranged the Solar System.

Now don't tell, Dearie, on your word
Of honor as a planet;
The cause of Mars's red face I've heard
Is booze! He's sure the gay old bird—
It's years since he began it."
Then burst forth Vega, "What's the use
Of Luna's mad endeavor
To change her figure and 'reduce'
When in one month—the silly goose—
She'll be as round as ever?

"There's Berenice! She's marcelled her hair!
Her cute dog-star she's leading.
Here kid—take Cassiopeia's Chair.
What news? You don't say! Did they dare?
Young Comet pinched for speeding?
Well! Well! I've, too, a tale to stir;
Now Venus is no pattern,
We all know that, but Jupiter
Is worse—I'm not much blaming her—
She has eloped with Saturn!

"Of course she's flirted lots, my dears,
But Saturn's been her 'steady.'
He has a bad 'case' it appears,
Old softy! Why he's had for years
A *choice of rings* all ready!"

"This Radio," I rejoiced, "what fun!
And cheaper than a movie."
Just then John's voice boomed like a gun,
"Wake up, old girl—it's half past one.
And put the cat out, Lovey."

Amazing Stories Quarterly, Fall/Winter 1932

Recognition
Enola Chamberlain

The Mars Man took the pilot's proffered gold,
Looked at the marking on it, heard it clink,
Half turned away as if he wished to think;
Then smiled, spread out his hands, let go their hold.
"By this," he said, "I know you're from the earth;
The only planet where there still remains
The caste of wealth to hold a race in chains—
The only place where gold exceeds man's worth."

Fantasy Book, July 1948

Evolution

Julia Boynton Green

Long have wise folk a baffling secret sought—
The mystery of human origins.
A theory rises—sinks; another wins
A transient credence. Some men will have naught
Of simian kin, nor bear the shocking thought
Of simple earthly sources of our sins
And virtues. These are valiant paladins.
But by slight hints may not deep truths be taught?

Often when strolling idly out of doors
The joy of upright carriage thrills me through—
As though in some dim past I'd gone "all-fours"!
And often speech, or victory in some test
Of wits, stirs quick surprise, a wonder new,
As though I'd once lacked language, groped, and guessed!

Amazing Stories, August 1931

Mutation
Lilith Lorraine

His mother bore him in the nuclear dawn
Deep in a cave beneath an iron sky
Lit by strange suns and moons that rose awry
And set at man's command. All things were pawn
To man except himself, and he was slave
To his own passions. Where the last bombs fell
He cowered deep within his steel-walled cell,
And mouldered in his radio-active grave.

And he whose sire had lived with sun and shower
Walked shambling where the great wheels noiseless droned,
Serving the dimming mind, the beast enthroned,
Until the soul shall waken to its power.
The monster clenched six fists beneath the sky,
Cursed with two mouths and glared with one red eye.

Super Science Stories, June 1951

Lost Earth
Rita Barr

The mountains rest their weary heads
Against the crimson sky
Beyond the brink of the black abyss
Where the broken planets lie—
Where silence is a cormorant,
Devouring every sound,
And verdure will never again caress
The wasted breast of the ground.
Once, there were eons when skies were blue
And the world was gold and green—
When the glad spheres sang in harmony,
And the star-lanes were serene.
Till a thing called Man in the latter days
Was impelled by a demon-curse
To pluck the fruit of the atom-tree,
And shatter the universe.
Are there new worlds borning in outer space,
To light the ebony void?
And will new stars rise in the paths of those
That the creature called Man destroyed?
Hold fast to your faith, you Elder Ones,
And pray to the gods you know
That hope did not die with the human-kind
On that lost earth—long ago.

Fantasy Book, July 1948

Out of Space
Dorothy Quick

She stared into the cauldron of the night.
Where wind lashed branches wove into a snare,
And fog rose out of a miasmic earth
Bringing strange music from she knew not where,
She could see nothing but the glinting light
Of eyes that made a pattern in the dark,
She did not know what evil gave them birth.
Swift winged as flinted arrows to a mark
They reached her heart. While in her ears the sound
Of beating music throbbed and louder grew.
The blackness ebbed like waves about her feet.
This was a terror no one ever knew.
This was an evil only she had found,
Nameless, and horrible from out of space.
She, at that moment, glimpsed where two worlds meet—
And tried, but could not turn her stricken face.

Weird Tales, May 1952

Chief Engineer
Lucrezia Reynard

Some day we who huddle in our
gadget-haunted hogans
at sub-zero temperatures
wishing for a comfortable leopard skin
to allay the fuel shortage
will presently—
snap on the light switch
and no light will come
will presently exhaust the last pint of gas
on a rutted highway
and leave the car there
in a vast steel graveyard
as a final monument
to free enterprise.
Someday our planes will fall from the heavens
like wounded birds
stretching their bat-winged skeletons
knee-deep in atom dust.
Yes, we shall presently
snap on a light-switch
and there will be no light.
Somebody—somewhere
has turned off the Master-Switch.

Fantasy Book, January 1950

Science and the Saucepans
Julia Boynton Green

How dangerous it is to live!
If we had known the peril
Of germs—the care we'd have to give
To keep each darned thing "sterile,"

We would have dodged being born I guess,
We would have stayed I'll wager
In uncomfortable nothingness
Up baiting Ursa Major.

Nothing we have to eat, it seems,
Is wholesome if it's tasty,
All sauces you must shun—and creams,
They make your color pasty.

You can't eat eggs or beans or meats
Or you invite "necrosis";
No starch or sweets, no snacks or treats,
For fear of "acidosis."

The lowly kraut ranks high today,
If you would be well fed you'll
Stow lots and lots of it away
And star it on your schedule.

Often, hid deep within our works,
Demanding circumspection,
Grim goggled M.D.'s find there lurks
A "focus of infection."

We must keep tab on vitamins
And calories and such like.
We pay for dietetic sins
In gripes that we don't much like.

As though we hadn't plagues enough
There's still that weird "milk culture."
Before I'd touch the loathsome stuff
I'd seek a swift sepulture!

I ask you, *What* shall be our meals?
Give that your contemplation.
There's left, this screed of mine reveals,
A microscopic ration.

A breakfast, I submit, of bran,
To dodge foes that beset us.
For lunch, five prunes: a prudent plan.
And if you'd add to life's brief span
Dine sparingly on lettuce.

Amazing Stories, June 1936

Because the Moon Is Far

Katherine Simons

Because the moon is far I have grown weary
    Of Earth and earthly things.
I find the same recurrent seasons dreary
    And crave Saturnian springs.

What nights are there of diamond-white desire
    Where Mercury has found
The stairways of the sun? What peaks aspire
    From Pluto's outer ground?

It may be, in the ghostly, frozen spinneys
    Of Neptune's sunless morn,
The flying serpent nests and that there whinnies
    The milk-white unicorn.

In slumber tangent to the arc of wonder
    I feel the fire hail
Of Jupiter and—through primeval thunder—
    I hear his dragons wail.

Let him who thinks he winnows truth from seeming
    And candleflame from star
Accept reality but leave me dreaming—
    Because the moon is far.

Weird Tales, November 1943

The Evil Star
Enola Chamberlain

Within the palace plane the guide was saying,
    "This is the earth, the last outpost of force.
Feel how her hate waves keep our space ship swaying,
    How anger buffets us from off our course."
The beings in the plane, with eyes that sifted
    Through fog and dark, looked down on man's abode.
They saw the earth, her lovely face uplifted,
    While war in hob-nailed boots across her strode.
Then suddenly the three-decked plane was sinking,
    "Weight of earth's fear. More power!" the captain cried.
Her rockets flashed—a new star brightly blinking—
    And men who saw her go were mystified.

Fantasy Book, July 1949

Siren Spotlight on Lilith Lorraine

Lilith Lorraine, one of many pseudonyms used by Mary Maud Dunn (1894–1967), was the single most important woman in speculative poetry before Ursula K. Le Guin started publishing poems in the 1970s, but I was a little worried that we wouldn't find anything of hers to print: To avoid becoming overwhelmed, we limited this book to professional magazines. That left fanzines out in the cold and jettisoned dozens of women out the airlock. We did choose a poem published in *Weird Tales* by Gertrude Wright, and it turns out this was likely Lorraine. (In various newspaper articles from the 1920s, as well as the 1920 census, her husband, Cleveland Lamar Wright, is mentioned as being married to Gertrude Wright.) And at the last minute we found *Fantasy Book*, a professional magazine whose poetry column she edited, which also featured some of her poetry.

Others have tried to piece together Lorraine's life story (please do check the endnotes), so I'll concentrate on her importance to poetry instead of, say, her arrest for running a sex cult and subsequent flight to Mexico to avoid prosecution (seriously, check those endnotes).

After publishing a handful of science fiction stories in pulp magazines in the late 1920s and early 1930s, she earned her place in the speculative poetry pantheon with a series of fanzines and semi-professional poetry journals. In 1943 she began editing *The Raven*, a poetry zine devoted to the legacy of Poe. She followed that a few years later with *Different*, which published both fiction and poetry, with an emphasis on speculative poetry. In 1950 she launched *Challenge*, the first speculative poetry magazine. It lasted only four issues before she folded it into *Different*. She later published *Flame*, a semi-professional poetry journal that published work by underground literary heroes Richard Brautigan and Charles Bukowski. Her 1952 collection *Wine of Wonder* was the first modern science fiction poetry book by a woman. She also wrote poetry textbooks and a psychology manual for poets.

Throughout her career, she worked to shape the very genre of poetry. Her Avalon Poetry Shrine, later the Avalon World Arts Academy, was dedicated to pushing back the forces of modernism in poetry and society in general. She dismissed modernist poetry, saying that its practitioners wanted "to indulge in weird distortions of the patterns of a poetry, merely for the sake of being different and not for any sane or logical reason, to attempt to disguise his emotional infancy, his intellectual anemia, and his spiritual poverty under the guise of linguistic gymnastics." Instead, she advocated easily understood, inspirational poetry that used classical forms to appeal to the widest possible audience.

Although she's forgotten now, Lorraine's importance to the field did not go unnoticed in her day. Clark Ashton Smith, probably the best of the *Weird Tales* poets, said, "Lilith Lorraine, poet and seer, walks intrepidly the ways that science has opened into the manifold infinities. She widens the scope of wonder into stars and atoms, into ulterior worlds and posterior ages."[1]

Michael W. Phillips Jr.

Notes

1. Joshua B. Buhs, "Lilith Lorraine as a Fortean," From an Oblique Angle, joshuablubuhs.com/blog/lilith-lorraine-as-a-fortean; Steve Sneyd, ed., introduction to *Time Grows Thin* (2009).

Some Secret Spell of the Long Ago
Historical Poems

We have to admit that this collection is incredibly white. We have one identifiably nonwhite poet. Readers, we tried! But we found that, as far as anyone knows, very, very few writers of color published in pulp horror or sci-fi magazines. The most notable example, Wallace Thurman, was a Black ghostwriter for several pulps, including *Ghost Stories*. But he's ineligible for inclusion here because we can't know whether he published poetry, and besides, he's a dude.[1] It's possible—no, probable—that more women of color wrote for the pulps. Some are probably hidden among the dozens of authors whose personal histories are lost, who used their initials instead of their full names, or who published under pseudonyms.

There's a significant history of Black people writing sci-fi and horror. Martin Delany's *Blake; or the Huts of America* is a pre–Civil War alternate history novel, and Pauline Hopkins's 1903 novel *Of One Blood* is an H. Rider Haggard–style "lost race" adventure story. Rudolph Fisher's 1932 novel *The Conjure-Man Dies* feels like a supernatural story until its more prosaic ending. And both W.E.B. du Bois and Zora Neale Hurston wrote sci-fi in the 1920s.

During the time period covered in this book, there were plenty of Black people writing sci-fi and horror stories—they just published it elsewhere. "I would expect that the absence of writers of color (in speculative fiction magazines) was due in part to the difficulty of breaking into a closed publishing circle," said Venetria K. Patton, a dean and professor of English, African American Studies, and Gender at the University of Illinois Urbana-Champaign. She mentioned the Harlem Renaissance, that flowering of Black art, literature, and music of the 1920s and early 1930s. The appearance of writers like Langston Hughes and Zora Neale Hurston in formerly white-only magazines was the result of a campaign by Civil Rights organizations to convince publishers to include work by Black writers. They sponsored prizes and made personal introductions to white editors. Absent those introductions to the staff of speculative fiction magazines, Black authors looked to other outlets for their work, a tendency Nigerian-Canadian horror novelist Felix I.D. Dimaro eloquently called "get in where you fit in." Black newspapers including the *Baltimore Afro-American* and the *Pittsburgh Courier*, which had nationwide distribution, printed pulp-style horror, sci-fi, and fantasy stories.[2] However, this collection spotlights poets of the pulps and does not include newspapers and mainstream magazines.

When I suggested that racism had little to do with the lack of writers of color because the editors couldn't have known the race of people sending in poems, Dimaro pointed out that Black people lived in Black neighborhoods, so the return address on a submission could have tipped off an editor that the submitter was Black. He also posited that editors might have rejected minority writers' work on the basis of the subject matter.

Besides, affluence matters. "Black women writers who could afford to write whatever they wanted were largely of the Black bourgeoisie and 'race women' committed to uplift," said Adrienne Brown, associate professor in the Departments of English and Race, Diaspora and Indigeneity at the University of Chicago. "Thus, they weren't writing sci-fi or horror."

There's less research about other races or ethnicities' relationship to pulps. James W. Bennett, a former American diplomat stationed in Shanghai, co-authored several stories with a Chinese author credited as Soong Kwen-Ling or Kwoen-Ling; two were published in *Weird Tales*, and the rest appeared in a collection called *Plum Blossoms and Blue Incense* (1926). But most research on Asian Americans and the pulps talks about them as *characters* in pulp fiction, but not as *writers* of it. They were probably out there, but we don't know who they were, aside from Gerald(ine) Chan Sieg.

American society was more overtly racist in the first half of the twentieth century than it is today. That showed up in the pages of the pulps. The first name that springs to mind is H.P. Lovecraft, whose opinions about eugenics, race-mixing, lynch mobs, even Hitler are well-documented both in his fiction and in his letters to other writers.[3]

As one of my grad school professors said, people in the past had choices about their beliefs and actions. Everyone—including pulp writers—had the option of being or becoming less racist. If someone *could* have known better, they *should* have known better, and it's valid to talk about the choices they made. Both Robert E. Howard and Clark Ashton Smith told Lovecraft to tone down his racist rhetoric. He didn't. He wasn't alone.

The racism in the pulps existed on a spectrum. Take *Oriental Stories*, a magazine in which a bunch of white folks wrote fantasy stories set in Asian countries. The most prolific poet in that rag was white dude Frank Owen, who wrote two dozen poems under the name (I can't believe I'm typing this) "Hung Long Tom." You won't find anything from *Oriental Stories* in this book.

Some of the poets we're including—Mary Elizabeth Counselman, Katherine van der Veer, Leah Bodine Drake, and others—wrote racist junk that we trashed immediately. Counselman, especially, wrote some unforgivable stuff. For just one example, her poem "Nostalgia" is about a woman who worries she might be part Asian because she dreams about incense and gongs (*what pagan taint of blood is in our line?*).

Further along the spectrum are poems by white women about BIPOC cultures. By today's standards, we would call that cultural appropriation; during the time it was written, it was more likely considered cultural appreciation. So we opted to include some of that work, if it seemed respectful of the culture it borrowed from.

We recognize that some of the poems in this section include appropriation. We include poems about ancient Egypt, Babylon, Easter Island, Aztec human sacrifice—all written by white ladies. Pieces of these poems might make you wince, but we think they include other traits of merit and are worthy of consideration.

Among this sea of white women, we close this section with a poem by Gerald(ine) Chan Sieg, the only identifiably nonwhite woman poet we could find who published in horror and sci-fi pulps. She's in this book twice, with verses that play around with her cultural heritage as a Chinese-American woman. Happily, it was hers to play around with.

Michael W. Phillips Jr.

The Heads on Easter Island
Leah Bodine Drake

We know that human hands carved these lean faces
And set them on the dark volcanic hill,
Not fiends or titans!—only brown-limbed races,
Mysterious, unknown, but mortal still.
Whoever made these gods once gave them homage,
Brought yams and sweet green cane at dusk or dawn,
Danced to the shaking drums in sea-birds' plumage,
And cried their names and loved them, and were gone.

Yet to what men have worshipped always clings
A sense of life unearthly . . . and there lies
A spell of power and of timeless things
In these sardonic lips and hooded eyes;
And awe takes hold of any traveler there,
Who feels these stones are sleeping—but aware!

Weird Tales, January 1949

Sic Transit Gloria
Brooke Byrne

These formless mounds of earth that lie
Beneath the blue, sun-ridden sky,
Had they but voice, would loudly cry
    "We are the walls of Babylon!

"We are the stones that formed the street
Whereon the drums of commerce beat,
And we the stones that felt the feet
    Of all the world in Babylon.

"We have been stained with wine and blood
And gold poured down us in a flood
To where Bel's sacred temple stood,
    The golden heart of Babylon.

"Such wealth as ours has never been,
Such power and gold and depths of sin;
They were accursed who entered in
    The hundred gates of Babylon.

"And yet there thronged through every gate
From every nation, tribe, and state,
The thousands who would laugh at Fate
    And pleasure taste in Babylon.

"This heap was once, in ages dim,
The Hanging Garden, reared by him
Who ruled us all, to please the whim
    Of Amytis of Babylon.

"We felt the pulse of power throb,
We heard the tortured captive sob,
And over us the loot-mad mob
    Swept howling into Babylon.

"We saw Belshazaar at his play,
O'er us the Persians felt their way,
And we were left at break of day
    To see the doom of Babylon."

The Persian swords are heaps of rust,
And glory dies, as all things must,
And crumbled stone and shifting dust
    Is all Time leaves of Babylon.

Weird Tales, November 1933

Kishi, My Cat
Alice I'Anson

Kishi, my Cat,
With glowing eyes
    And softly flowing tail,
Did you love to dream
On a broidered mat
    While the desert stars grew pale?
Did you drowse at the feet of Ishtar, queen
    Of the Land of Ancient Guile?
Did she mimic you with her haughty mien
    And her strange Sumerian smile?

Kishi, my Cat,
I feel tonight
    Some bond betwixt us twain
That dates far back
To a time like that,
    To the great Belshazzar's reign.
You were the pet of the royal bride,
    I was chief of her dancing-maids. . . .
They buried us, too, when Ishtar died,
    And we followed her to the Shades!

Weird Tales, October 1932

A Vase from Araby

Leah Bodine Drake

Shaped like a tear-drop, pale as haze
Down where the mirage cities stand,
Here is the blue enamel vase
Brought overseas from the fabled land.

Stoppered with turquoise, scribed around
With golden symbols that curve and flow
Like a guardian serpent, the flask is bound
In some secret spell of the long ago.

If curious fingers should break the seal
What would be found in its narrow hold:
Poison to murder, or herbs to heal?
Attar of roses, or dust of gold?

Beware! . . . In a cloud as black as shame
Amazed eyes might see a Form appear,
With furious wings and hair of flame. . . .
The Djinni for ages imprisoned here!

Weird Tales, March 1943

Teotíhuacán
Alice I' Anson

I sing of pagan rites that long ago
Ruled the great city lying far below
The twin volcanoes' hoary bridge of snow—
    I sing the Song of Teotíhuacán!

Deep is the womb of Time in which I see
The drama of a dead idolatry!—
I hear old voices chanting now in me
    The mystic Song of Teotíhuacán!

"The red dawn shimmers on Tezcoco's lake,
O City of the Priests, awake, awake!
It is another Feast Day of the Snake,
    The Serpent God of Teotíhuacán!

"Behold the flaming signal in the skies!
The dawn is red!—today a victim dies!
O hear, O hear his agonizing cries,
    Great Serpent God of Teotíhuacán!

"Upon the stone his writhing form is laid—
His blood spurts redly from the 'itxli' blade—
With his dripping heart an offering is made,
    To the mighty God of Teotíhuacán!"

Shadows of centuries! still they grow apace
While Mystery hovers o'er the solemn place
Whose ruins whisper in this year of grace:
    "Where is the God of Teotíhuacán?"

O Souls that cross again the yawning deep
While round these monuments the lizards creep,
I feel your ghostly contact as you keep
    Your vigils in old Teotíhuacán!

O Sprit Guardians of this grim terrain,
Has Karma bound us with the selfsame chain?
Did I, too, worship at that gory fane
    Long years agone . . . in Teotíhuacán?

Weird Tales, November 1930

The Spirit-Boats
Minna Irving

Within the many-chambered tomb
For Tut-ankh-Amen built,
Among the alabaster jars,
The faience and the gilt,
Were placed the spirit-boats designed
To bear his soul away
To happy shores by Horus blest
With everlasting day.

Pink shallops far more fit to hold
Young Loves perfumed and curled
Than navigate the dreary dark
And haunted underworld,
Light fairy vessels that should rock
On waters laced with foam,
By sunny isles or emerald woods
Where Pan was wont to roam.

No doubt the ancient monarch hoped
On blue Egyptian nights
To steer his bark to mundane parts
And taste of old delights,
Between the lotus-lilies drift
Along the star-lit Nile,
And play the sistrum for his queen
While basking in her smile.

Behold! above the dusky hills
The new moon's silver boat
Upon its bright celestial way
Serenely certain float.
Who knows? Mark Antony its course
From sky to earth may guide,
To visit once again the scene
Where Cleopatra died.

Famous Fantastic Mysteries, December 1939

Candles

Dorothy Quick

Bring candles red and candles white
To light my lord, the King, tonight:
Candles red for his heart's true worth
Flaming for him, who rules the earth;
Candles white for the soul of him,
And never let their light grow dim;
Candles white and candles red
To guide him to the bridal bed.

Bring candles blue and candles green
To light my lady fair, the Queen:
Candles blue for her trusting eyes
And for the faith that in them lies;
Candles green for the land she brings,
That join her sovereign Lord's, the King's;
Candles blue and candles green
To light the chamber of the Queen.

Candles red, green, white and blue,
All burning with a steady hue.
White her body, red her mouth,
Green her lands, both north and south;
Red the passion of his kiss,
White her yielding unto this;
Blue the panels of her room,
Blue the overhanging doom.

White the moonlight where she lies,
Blue the terror in her eyes;
Red the blood on the King's hands—
Fair and broad were her green lands.
Light candles tall and candles white
To speed the Queen's soul on its flight.
Bring candles tall and candles black
To light the King on his way back.

Weird Tales, January 1934

Reflections of an Egyptian Princess While Being Interred
Edith Ogutsch

I lie here in state, at Karnak
My body is dressed like a bride
The coffin is cheerfully painted
But for me it is dark inside.

The priests and the slaves are wailing
They place a jar at my head
The viscera drawn through my nostrils
And preserved, of the newly dead.

Provisions are put round my coffin
To lighten my arduous way
I'll linger a little while longer
The Gods please forgive my delay.

I think of the joys of childhood
The leisurely days by the Nile
The warm autumn nights in the vineyards
My father's affectionate smile.

I long for the arms of my lover
The bliss that we shared 'neath the moon
My heart cries a prayer to Isis
To let me be born again soon.

The mourners have left—I'm frightened
Supposing the priests aren't right?
Perhaps there is only the one life
And this the eternal night.

The striving, the struggling onwards
The learning, the drawing each breath
Does it end right here in this chamber
Or do we go on after death?

I lie here forgotten, at Karnak
The centuries slowly creep by
A princess of ancient Egypt
Not living, unable to die.

Weird Tales, January 1954

Reincarnation
Gerald Chan Sieg

Throughout the ages I have known
Your lovely laughter and your tears,
Your fingers locking with my own.
I saved you from a dinosaur,
Then lost you till the spinning years
Returned you in the Trojan War.

Together we endured the whips
Of pagan Rome and, singing, died;
Together watched the Tartar ships
Unloading silk from dim Cathay
Which softly robed you as my bride.
(A thousand years are but a day.)

I found you next in Aragon,
A maiden hid in costly lace;
And later—ah, sweet Puritan
In your prim bonnet, sober dress,
Who went with courage in your face
To dare with me a wilderness!

Your mind cannot recall the past.
You would be frightened if you knew
What powers, dark, eternal, vast,
I have controlled throughout the years
To keep the essence that is you:
Your lovely laughter and your tears!

Weird Tales, September 1941

Siren Spotlight on Gerald Chan Sieg

When compiling historical information of any sort, especially about marginalized populations, it's easy to overlook the very information you need: Consider Geraldine Chan Sieg (1909–2005), who wrote under the name "Gerald Chan Sieg." It would be easy for collectors or researchers looking for female writers to miss her—in fact, Eric Leif Davin's otherwise indispensable *Partners in Wonder* omits her.

Sieg's only genre work appears to be four poems in *Weird Tales*, though she was a prolific poet. She wrote stories for *The Atlantic* and published the 12-page *The Chinese Christmas Box* in 1970. She is also considered the first female poet of Savannah, Georgia, and her parents were Savannah's first Chinese American family.

"Her poems provide a window into the world of Chinese immigrants, including dealing with loneliness, homesickness, nostalgia, and racial discrimination; embracing family life, community well-being, and the beautiful southern landscape; and becoming contributing members of the larger Savannah society," according to The Association of Chinese Americans for Social Justice's website (as translated from the original Chinese via Google Translate, adjusted for clarity).

Sieg published her first poem in high school, in 1927, which won a prize from the Georgia Poetry Society. A year later, the society invited her to join. She held most society offices, including president.

The society honored Sieg in 1978 with the Gerald Chan Sieg Award, which was its second award ever named for a living person. In a story about the award, the *Savannah Morning News-Press* wrote, "Diminutive but by no means retiring, delicate but hardly shy, Gerald Chan Sieg is the embodiment of the articulate, cultured, self-made woman. Assertive, not strident, and fascinating but never self-centered, she has been 'a suffragette since the age of seven.' Her purpose is freedom of expression, and her recent honor attests to the realization of that goal for her."

Jaclyn Youhana Garver

Notes

I would like to thank Bobby Derie, proprietor of the blog Deep Cuts in a Lovecraftian Vein (deepcuts.blog), for his invaluable assistance in researching the introduction to this chapter, and Timaeus Bloom for reading an early draft.

1. David Earle, "Black Writers of the Pulps: The Case of Wallace Thurman and Harlem Stories," Boozehounds & Bookleggers, boozehoundsblog.com/pulps/2015/10/6/black-writers-for-the-pulps-the-case-of-wallace-thurman-and-harlem-stories
2. Brooks E. Hefner's *Black Pulp: Genre Fiction in the Shadow of Jim Crow* (2022) is essential reading on this subject.
3. Aja Romano, "Lovecraftian Horror—and the Racism at Its Core—Explained," vox.com/culture/21363945/hp-lovecraft-racism-examples-explained-what-is-lovecraftian-weird-fiction

How Dream the Mad?
Poems of Dreams and Nightmares

During a particularly stressful time in life, I had my first—and, so far, only—waking nightmare.

I had gone to bed five or ten minutes prior. I lay on my back, on the left side of the bed. My right elbow was bent, so my right fist curled loosely at my face, which was turned to the right, my cheek against the cool pillowcase. I had found the earliest stage of sleep, where you're beautifully relaxed but still alert.

Then I heard a noise.

I laid there and listened for a few beats as the noise continued. I tried to place the sound, which was even, airy, quiet.

It sounded like . . . breathing?

I turned my head to my left and saw a face. I blinked, figuring the face for a weird hallucination. It didn't fade. I rubbed my eyes. Still, the face hovered.

It was my husband's face—just his face—but it was dark blue. He had horns. And fangs, which I saw because the face was smiling. Its expression never changed. The face just floated there, watching me and breathing.

I rubbed my eyes some more, blinked hard. Still my demon husband watched, breathed. I tried to back up, to get further from the face, but I succeeded only in pressing my head further into the down of the pillow.

So I took a deep breath . . . and I screamed my goddamn head off.

My husband—my actual husband, with a full body, without horns and fangs—burst into the room and flipped on the light. I kept screaming. I looked at him, then I looked to where his blue face had hovered. At him, toward the space with the face, which faded away slowly with the light. Back and forth, back and forth, screaming the whole time. At some point, I think a piece of me hovered above my body, like, "Sweetie, stop screaming. Stop it. What is wrong with you?"

Which is all to say: Sleep can be a terrifying, horrifying thing.
Just look at Sara Henderson Hay's "Night Terror":

Its little gasping flame is all
We have, to guard and keep the sill
From things that wait, close-cloaked about
In darkness, where the shadows sprawl—

Most of the poets in this chapter treat the subject of sleep similarly: It's a place where we're *doomed and mad* (Dorothy Marie Peterkin), where *every hour my senses cower / And writhe the whole night through* (Edna Bell Seward).

And why not? The umbrella of sleep covers a slew of tropes and topics that are wrought for the horrific: the monster under the bed, the witching hour, things that go bump in the night, the thing in the closet, the bogeyman. Sleep leaves us defenseless, without guard, tender.

The following chapter does have a few poems that look on sleep with a kinder eye, including Katherine Van Der Veer's "Place Names"; while it acknowledges sleep's *haunting shadow of a pain*, the poem also pays heed to happy dreams. Without leaving our bed, sleep lets us travel; gaze upon mountain peaks, fountains, and gardens; and pass everyday people in the sweet mundanity of their lives: *What magic lies about a whispered name / That sends one headlong out of space and time.*

Hopefully, wherever you land, it's free of flame—and blue-faced spouses with horns.

Jaclyn Youhana Garver

Suspicion
Harriet A. Bradfield

If this is dew on my fingers,
Why do I feel such dread?
What do the shadows whisper?
Why does the water run red?

What has the night been plotting
While all were drugged with sleep?
This phantom clinging so tightly—
Why does it silently weep?

Weird Tales, November 1953

Clair de Lune
Minnie Faegre Knox

O never ye sleep in the moonlight,
    My pious old Granny would say,
For sleepers, bewitched by the moonlight,
    With madness thereafter are fay.

But why should I sleep when the moon shines,
    And waste all her beauty away?
There's more to be done when the moon shines
    Than slumber in houses and pray.

My body I'll bathe in the moon-rays,
    My mantle of dew shall be spun.
Encrowned in a nimbus of moon-rays,
    I'll dance till the night flee the sun.

And if I should yield to the moonbeams,
    Laid low by weird malison's harm,
Let me sleep 'neath the turn in the moonbeams,
    Enthralled by the night's silver charm.

Weird Tales, May 1928

The Doomed
Dorothy Marie Peterkin

How dream the mad? My dreams have been to me
All that the friends I longed for could not be;
Clearer were dreams than hard realities;
Sweeter were dreams than piper's melodies.

How dream the mad? For if I can not dream,
I were much better dead. Will shadows seem
Real to me then, and winds that blow,
Bodied companions? Only madmen know.

Weird Tales, June 1929

Sleepers
Dorothy Quick

Out of the night what laughter sprayed the air
Cadenced and fell into some timeless void
A vibrant instant, then no longer there?
One sleeper heard it and his sleep destroyed
Awoke in rage, another did not care,
And still another, hearing music gleam
Across the starlight from he knew not where,
Was drunken with the magic of a dream.

Weird Tales, September 1951

Why Was My Dream So Real?
June Power Reilly

Why was the dream I had last night so real?
    Why should I wake with startled breath, a scream
Upon my lips? For I could shuddering feel
    The hot flames lick my cheeks. If it were dream
Why should I have the old remembered pain?
    Where came the banners? Where the soldiered place?
Where have I known the stake and jeers that rain
    Like pointed stones? Where have I known disgrace?

Ah, dreams are made of things so misty, more
    Like webs of spiders, or a touch of thought;
But this was something deep, an opened door
    That opened half-way, then the hinges caught.
When just about to hear them shout my name
    I woke, with agony of burning flame.

Weird Tales, July 1935

The Murderer
Edna Bell Seward

Night is the time to drink the wine
Of sleep—it conscience frees;
But a guilty soul must quaff the bowl
That's full of bitter lees.
It's brewed in hell where devils dwell
—I drink its loathsome rue—
Then every hour my senses cower
And writhe the whole night through.

My murd'rous hands are once more spanned
Around my victim's throat;
His cries I hear of mortal fear
While round me devils gloat;
Upon my breast with leering jest
REMORSE lays heavily—
And all too late I see the gate
Of hell awaiting me.

To God I pray to bring the day—
When Furies 'round me scream—
Pray for an hour from their power
In sleep—that has no dream.
Night is the time to drink the wine
Of sleep—it conscience frees;
But a guilty soul must quaff a bowl
That's full of bitter lees.

Weird Tales, March 1924

Place Names
Katherine van der Veer

What magic lies about a whispered name
    That sends one headlong out of space and time,
That lights within a clear and lonely flame
    To burn unseen on some forgotten shrine?

"I brought this fan from Spain," was all she said—
    Out of a courtyard, cobblestoned and white,
The click of castanets, a faint guitar,
    Came on a scented wind across the night.

I saw great mountain peaks, snow-crowned and stern,
    Fountains and gardens, rose-hung, trimly set,
The shimmering Genil winding far below
    Granada's Moorish pile and parapet.

A peasant breaking stone beside the road,
    With leathery hands, soft dust upon his hair,
Toiling to keep his tiny whitewashed home,
    Smiled as I passed, intangible as air.

So frail a thing, this journey that I went
    In insubstantial form, there fell again
The veil that hides the present from the past
    And threw the haunting shadow of a pain.

Weird Tales, January 1934

The Suicide's Awakening
Gertrude Wright

Spirits of fire, who dwell in the deep,
Why do ye torture me out of my sleep?

Angels of darkness who float in the flame,
Why are ye moaning and calling my name?

Ghosts of the unredeemed, fallen from grace,
Why do your crimson wings flap in my face?

Demons that circle under the wave,
Why are ye howling over my grave?

Back, ye fiends, back again, to the unknown;
I am a dead thing: leave me alone.

Cold are my limbs and departed my breath;
I am not living, but this is not death.

Weird Tales, May 1925

Night Terror
Sara Henderson Hay

Lie still—the phantom stars are clear,
The moon is white against the snow—
Ah, Mary Mother, make Them fear
Even this candle's feeble glow—
Make Them afraid to enter here!

Its little gasping flame is all
We have, to guard and keep the sill
From things that wait, close-cloaked about
In darkness, where the shadows sprawl—
What should we do if it went out?—
Lie still . . .

Weird Tales, July 1930

Siren Spotlight on Harriet A. Bradfield

Harriet A. Bradfield (1899–1953) does not, upon first inspection, seem to be a writer one would find within the pages of *Weird Tales*, which published six of her poems; nearly 200 poems, meanwhile, appeared in various romance magazines over the course of her life and posthumously. Bradfield's résumé includes English lit and writing teacher, *Writer's Digest* columnist, editor of *Cupid's Diary* magazine, and managing editor for the comic book *Love Romances*. In the latter role, she insisted on being the first reader for all submissions, and she enjoyed reading the letters that came with manuscripts; she liked to know her writers. Occasionally, submitters would address her as Mr. Bradfield and attempt to flirt, which she always got a kick out of.

The Author & Journalist trade journal once called her an editor "you want to know."

While the bulk of her career skewed toward romance, Bradfield clearly had at least a dabbling interest in eerie delights: When she was 18, she wrote to the novelist and poet Hamlin Garland, who shared her hometown of La Crosse, Wisconsin. "It seems to strange to see in a book the names of all the places so familiar to me," she wrote. "We pass your old home often in the summer, and the dark, rambling house is one I have always loved to believe was ghost-haunted. Is it really, I wonder?"

And the circumstances of her death seem tailored for the dark and unfortunate: Bradfield died in her Washington D.C. home on a Monday. She was not found until Thursday, after friends wondered where she'd been.

Jaclyn Youhana Garver

I Weave My Death
Poems of Death and Dying

Horror in the first half of the twentieth century was pretty tame by modern standards. A lot had to be left to the imagination: Compare the eerie, almost dreamlike pace and suggestiveness of *Nosferatu* (1922) with, I don't know, *Hostel*. The same can be said about horror literature, which didn't drip with much viscera until the 1970s.

Though there's plenty of death in this book, it's mild-mannered. Ghosts abound, but the writers don't usually go into grisly detail about how the ghosts became ghosts. Beware of vampires, but don't expect these fanged friends to rip out any throats or guzzle blood. That restraint is a feature, not a bug.

But as I mentioned: *so many dead people* in this book. Lots of murderers, too. We encounter the dead before, or during, or after their deaths; and we meet their killers, consumed by guilt. Instead of vivid descriptions of gouts of blood and shattered skulls, the authors danced around the subject—a delicate ballet of hint and implication that makes the loss of life hit harder. Page Cooper's "A Curse" (not to be confused with her poem "The Curse," elsewhere in the book) is a bitter, vindictive malediction against a murderer; though we don't know what he did, we know that it's bad enough that he'll spend eternity *Parched with lust for a phantom kiss, / Faint for the joy (he) never knew.*

Sometimes death comes along with a hefty dose of black comedy: Leah Bodine Drake's "Six Merry Farmers" is an amusing, alcohol-fueled romp through the Kentucky hills—until the final line drops like a Monday morning hangover.

Sometimes death comes laden with spite: The narrator of Louise Garwood's "The Living" bids venomous goodbye to a rival whose *lips and eyes / are food to make the rose more fair*; and Marie W. Linné's "Mementos" is the "Missing You" by John Waite of pulp horror poetry. I wouldn't dream of spoiling a single line!

And sometimes, death is bleak and relentless: Cristel Hastings's "Penalty," a chronicle of a hanging, is as terrifying as anything Eli Roth or Ti West could imagine, unbuoyed by wistfulness or hope.

Don't get me wrong: I love extreme, gross-out horror. (I've published Paula D. Ashe, Lor Gislason, and Felix I.D. Dimaro, all of whom are experts in making readers lose their lunch.) There's a through-line from Poe, to Lovecraft, to the women in this collection, and that line continues through Ashe and Gislason and Dimaro. Because the payoff—the splatter, the guts on the concrete—is much more delicious (ew) if it's earned, if it's teased out until the reader just can't stand it anymore.

That's something the best horror writers understand.

Michael W. Phillips Jr.

Penalty
Cristel Hastings

Veiled was the moon and gray the sea,
And white was the thing that stared at me,
For a dead man hung on a gallows tree—
Veiled was the moon and gray the sea.

Black was the hood they tied on his head
As he woke from sleep and left his bed,
Within that dread hour to hang dead—
Black was the hood they tied on his head.

Still was the room where the hangman stood
As quietly as a hangman could,
And little there seemed in this world of good—
Still was the room where the hangman stood.

Loud was the voice of the wind outside
Where trees bent low and a raging tide
Sobbed because a man had died—
Loud was the voice of the wind outside.

Dark is the room where the gallows stood,
Empty the limp and tear-wet hood,
And little is left in the night of good—
Dark is the room where the gallows stood.

Weird Tales, November 1932

Mist on the Meadows
Marion Doyle

Strange portents there are—
    What gain to deny them?—
'Twixt twilight and dawning;
    What use to defy them?

And now you contend this
    Is mist on the meadow—
I never heard of a
    Mist casting shadow.

It is not mist, but
    The uneasy dead
Trailing their long shrouds
    Low overhead,

Blurring the high moon
    And blotting the stars,
Caught in the Judas-trees—
    Death's avatars.

This is unholy:
    If you would be
Inviolate
    Eternally,
Turn you about
    And flee—
        And flee!

Weird Tales, November 1934

Six Merry Farmers
(A Kentucky Tale)
Leah Bodine Drake

Six merry farmers
    Lurching from a tavern,
Swaying down a village street
    At midnight, arm in arm;
One tried to kiss the moon
    Shining in a puddle,
Went to sleep and snored there
    Miles from his farm.

Five merry farmers!
    Two got to fighting,
The Sheriff came by
    And hauled them off to jail.
The fourth roared a gospel-hymn
    And went to look for women;
The fifth thought of little lambs
    And sat down to wail.

The last merry farmer
    Weaving up the hill-road
Met an old witch-woman
    Who was anything but fair.
When he gravely cursed her
    She up and be-spelled him
And what had been a farmer
    Was a wild buck hare!

Two merry farmers
    Riding home in dawn-light,
One sees a wild buck hare
    And lets off his gun:
Five merry farmers
    Sleeping off their merriment
And one not so merry
    Lying dead in the sun.

Weird Tales, September 1953

The Living
Louise Garwood

She can not smell those roses.
She can not even see.
Take them off her coffin!
Give them to me!
Henceforth her lips and eyes
    are food to make the rose more fair,
And when she blooms I'll take her
    and wear her in my hair.

Weird Tales, September 1929

A Curse
Page Cooper

When the last black, vampire hour of night
    Sucks at the throat of the dying moon,
Or the brask sun scorches with avid light
    The tremulous, fevered flesh of noon,
Through ice or blizzard or bitter hiss
    Of rain, you'll seek for the love you slew,
Parched with lust for a phantom kiss,
    Faint for the joy you never knew.

Weird Tales, January 1949

Fate
Thelma E. Johnson

I know a land of beauty and of peace:
    Serene it lies, beyond the gates of death,
    Remote and holy, free from any breath
Of earthly winds and rain that never cease;
And there with you, beloved, I would walk
    Deep in the windless solitude sublime,
    A child of music and of careless rime,
And oh, how new and strange would be our talk!

But there is one who still withholds the key:
    He stands unmoved beside the marble gate,
    A veiled, colossal figure—is it Fate
Or only Death that chills the heart of me?
    Beloved, will I walk with you alone
    In that far land, between the gates of stone?

Weird Tales, October 1929

Forgetful Hour
Yetza Gillespie

When time wears thin
As the shadows lying,
And the whippoorwills call
For the souls of the dying,

When the bitter moon wears
A star on her horns,
And the heart in your breast
Remembers thorns,

Be wise, and touch iron!
Put salt on your bread,
Lest some of the Ancient
Forget they are dead.

Weird Tales, March 1946

A Grave

Lilla Poole Price

O, bury me under the soft, blue waves,
    'Mid the swirl of the billows free;
        Let me find sweet rest
        'Neath their foam-tipp'd crest
    In the depths of the murmuring sea.

No bell shall be toll'd with its mournful sound,
    No funeral pall shall be spread,
        But a solemn hush
        And a soft, sad rush
    As the waters close over my head.

A tangle of seaweed shall be my shroud,
    And a mound of coral my bier;
        The voice of the sea
        Shall my requiem be,
    And my sleep will be tranquil here.

No roses nor lilies may deck my grave,
    Nor marble shall mark my rest,
        But the wonderful flow'rs
        Of the ocean bow'rs
    Shall lovingly twine o'er my breast.

Then bury me under the sad sea waves,
    Where the winds moan soft and low;
        Let the tears that are shed
        For the deep-cover'd dead
    With the shimmering wavelets flow.

Weird Tales, June 1926

Mementos
Marie W. Linné

I will not haunt you after I am dead;
　My wistful, sad, unsatisfied wraith
Shall not be lingering near these streets we tread,
　These walls that look so much on love and death;
My hungry laughing eyes, the words we said
Shall no way haunt you after I am dead. . . .

Oh, I'll have other things than these to do;
　I'll find a deep depression in a hill,
And to the wind's white songs, the drip of dew,
　Call all lost, joyous hearts to dance their fill,
So passers-by shall wonder, pausing there,
Remembering joy before man knew despair.

And I will keep a tame wind for my own,
　And if I break your musings, now and then,
Riding by, through some lamplit dusk, alone,
　You will remember lightly, once again,
A snatch of song, a vanished jest or two. . . .
No, but for these, I'll not come back to you.

Weird Tales, May 1934

The Curtain
Nina Wilcox Putnam

The painted face in the looking-glass
    Stares back at Harlequin;
There is a noise outside and a smell of gas,
    But he sits quite still with mechanical grin.

The gay crowd pours from the theater door
    Into the rain and sleet;
But Harlequin sits quite still before
    They robe him in a winding sheet.

The Thrill Book, July 1, 1919

Pattern
Dorothy Quick

The child was weaving
A strange and terrible pattern,
Beyond his conceiving
In the stark room of a slattern.

His eyes never strayed
From the taut web of his making;
He was not dismayed
Though his little hands were shaking

Yet he kept weaving
The dark and horrible design;
He had no believing
But the silken skeins were thin and fine.

The child was tired,
Yet his fingers flew fast as birds;
His cheeks were fired.
Still his trembling lips spoke no words.

"What are you weaving?"
A stranger asked with quickened breath.
Without deceiving
The child replied: "I weave my death."

Weird Tales, July 1950

Siren Spotlight on Dorothy Quick

Dorothy Quick (1896–1962) received a telegram from Mark Twain on her twelfth birthday. He asked, "Would you like an elephant or 10,000 monkeys for your birthday?" She replied that, instead, she'd like his books. He obliged, but he included a little white elephant in the gift, which inspired her to collect elephants throughout her life.

Quick is the most-published woman poet in *Weird Tales*. Unfortunately, as is often the case, much of the available information about Quick comes from her connection to men—such as her friendship with Twain. Which makes it difficult to learn more about her biography.

We know she wrote several poetry collections. She was also a novelist, newspaper columnist, and story writer. Her friendship with Twain inspired her memoir, *Enchantment: A Little Girl's Friendship with Mark Twain*, which was later adapted into the 1991 movie *Mark Twain and Me*. The two met when she was 11, on an ocean liner traveling to New York from England. Twain asked Quick which of his novels she liked best; she said she liked how Tom Sawyer got his fence whitewashed.

In his later years, Twain was lonely and often invited friends to visit him. According to a *New York Times* review of Quick's memoir, "Having reached the age of grandparenthood without having any grandchildren, he recruited some, among them the group of little girls he called his 'Angel Fish.' Dorothy Quick was one of them." *Enchantment* includes all the letters Quick received from Twain.

Jaclyn Youhana Garver

This Hot, Unhallowed Lust for Beauty
Poems of Lust and Longing

Every poem is a love poem—even the ones with dead things that crawl, lurk, and stink. Weep, bleed, and creep.

I started writing horror in adulthood, though I've been a No. 1 fan since much, much earlier, maybe since the time I started penning ridiculous, elementary love poems. And I think—I know—that the Venn diagram of love poetry and horror poetry overlaps much more than you might think: We conjure the dead because we miss those we lost. We murder our lovers because they scorned us for another, and we're terrifically bad at dealing with rejection and heartbreak. We move into haunted houses because we're broke and truly believe the huge-but-creepyass old pile of wood (and what the hell is up with that attic??) in the countryside is best for our family.

Which is all to say, it's no surprise that so many horror and horror-adjacent poems from the pulp era are preoccupied with love and all its forms and effects: jealousy (*Hawk-like watch your lovely bride / Till she sleeps safe at your side*), desire (*And she longed for the touch of his icy lips / Though she knew that one kiss would kill.*) and lost love:

> But you and I are changed.
> We who knew light
> And sunny laugher in this garden place
> Are shadows moving in a shadowy night.

We write about the topics of our obsession, the things about which we can't not write. I suspect musicians feel the same. And sculptors. Painters. Dancers. If you make art, you are compelled to do so by instinct, that same force that ensures babies can breathe and blink.

And how do we ID what those obsessions are? They're what we dream of in sleep and when work gets too boring, or the sky looks too blue, or we pass a waft of cologne or candle or lilac in the type of restaurant with white tablecloths or cheap beer. Every poem is a love poem because *a dream may live through a thousand years, / And our love was a dream begun / When I was a child.*

I could argue that all the poems in this entire collection are love poems because who are these pulp horror poets but women in love with the macabre and the inexplicable? The rope connecting romantic love to horror is thick: Each genre often boasts an element of the forbidden or something lost. There's the fear of something precious and beloved changing its mind with new information and experiences. There's longing, and the desperate things we'll do to satiate it:

> Demon Lover, Demon Lover
> What else can I do?
> I have whispered awful things
> Calling out to you.
> I have made a waxen man
> And bound it to my heart,
> Burned the the devil's candle,—
> Still you stay apart.

And when a heart is broken—or longing, or lonely, or manic—there's comfort in reading about the unholy unions that Dorothy Quick, Maisie Nelson, and Page Cooper sing about in the following pages.

These poems, like any meaningful piece of writing that can leave a scar (or maybe a lipstick smear or bite marks, ahem), whisper "You're not the only one."

Even if it's coming beyond the grave, what better message can possibly exist?

Jaclyn Youhana Garver

Quest Unhallowed

Page Cooper

Mortal lips will never touch you,
Mortal eye or hand or thigh or breast
Give you comfort of delight of loving,
Give you ecstasy or rest.

Thrall to phantom lips that sear you,
Burn your trembling flesh with bliss designed
For the angels, eyes whose lonely glory
Strikes you impotent and blind.

Stumbling through your finite paces
Hounded by a dream, you'll pray to die,
End this hot unhallowed lust for beauty
Mortals may not live to spy.

Weird Tales, March 1945

Demon Lover
Harriet A. Bradfield

Guard your bride and watch her well,
Lest a creature, freed from hell,
Gaze upon her virgin face,
Seek her out with gruesome grace;
Cast a spell upon her heart,
Then with fiendish joy depart.

If she's felt the demon spell,
She must follow, though to hell;
Hear you call her, but too late,
Leaving you to tortured wait.
Hawk-like watch your lovely bride
Till she sleeps safe at your side.

Weird Tales, May 1948

The White Sands of Bridesrun Beach
M. Ludington Cain

On Bridesrun beach the sands are white,
And here, the shore folk say,
A maid should go in the moon's pale light
On the eve of her wedding day.

She will know that her lover is true, as she
Runs barefoot on the sands,
For three young men will come out of the sea
And run to clasp her hands—

Three young gods with seaweed hair
And shoulders that gleam in the light. . . .
If her lover is true, they will leave her there
And vanish in the night.

But if unworthy her lover be,
The three will capture her. . . . Then
She will vanish with them out, out in the sea
And never be heard of again!

'Tis an idle thing that the legend tells,
But the shore folk swear 'tis so . . .
(Tomorrow will hear my wedding bells
And my love is true I know). . . .

The sands of Bridesrun beach are white,
(As white as my bridal veil) . . .
I wish I had courage to go there tonight—
Or never had heard the tale!

Fantastic Novels Magazine, June 1951

Garden at Lu

Gerald Chan Sieg

Cinnamon petals drop upon the air.
The night is still.
There is no sound but footsteps of the wind
Walking softly on a far off hill.
(How dim the night and still.)

All is the same: the ivy cool and dark
Against the moon-washed wall,
The little bamboo bridge, the sycamore
With branches lifted lonely, pale and tall.
(How lonely, pale and tall.)

Upon the pool the lily leaves encircle
A flower newly blown.
The long reeds watch the watered stars.
A golden fin goes gleaming and is gone.
(How quickly it is gone.)

All is the same. But you and I are changed.
We who knew light
And sunny laugher in this garden place
Are shadows moving in a shadowy night.
(How dim and long the night.)

Give me your hand. O let us softly move,
O softly move and slow,
Two shadows out of time who pause a while
To look on what we cherished long ago.
(How many aeons ago.)

Weird Tales, March 1942

Enduring
Maisie Nelson

She was the child of a rose and flame,
    A creature with sloe-black eyes,
And a mad flame-soul in her white rose breast,
    And a red mouth soft with sighs;
For she dreamed of the son of the old Frost King,
    So beautiful, pale and chill;
And she longed for the touch of his icy lips,
    Though she knew that one kiss would kill.

Oh, the years have fled, and the rose is dead,
    And the flame is an ash of gray,
And the ermine cloak of the old Frost King
    Is tattered and torn away;
But a dream may live through a thousand years,
    And our love was a dream begun
When I was a child of a rose and flame
    And you were the Frost King's son.

Weird Tales, September 1940

On Lake Lagore
Dorothy Gold

On Lake Lagore, when moonbeams glance
And glimmer on the black expanse,
The deep-drowned shadows rise and dance
    Under the cypress trees.

Who passes on the road beneath
The moss-hung branches holds his breath,
As one who looks on grisly death
    Shudders at what he sees.

But when the other shadows wake,
My lover rises from the lake,
And comes to me for love's sweet sake
    From out his watery bed.

So I, though others watch no more
The moon on haunted Lake Lagore,
Walk nightly here, and on the shore
    Keep vigil with the dead.

Weird Tales, November 1943

Strange
Dorothy Quick

He had been to the far places
And heard the music of distant spheres,
So the home hearth could never hold him
Or other music attract his ears.

He had looked into dark waters
And seen strange tides on a stranger shore
So never could his own beach hold him
Who had been far, who had seen more.

He had kissed strange lips in other places
And known strange loves on his distant way
So the arms that were his could not hold him
Whose spirit was restless and would not stay.

There's no peace for the man who at home abides
When he's known strange places, strange lips and tides.

Dark of the Moon anthology

Demon Lover

Dorothy Quick

Demon Lover, Demon Lover,
Will you never come?
I have walked thrice widdershins,
Bitten my own thumb.
I have spilled three drops of blood
And sung the song of shame,
Called to you with longing,
Named the dreadful name.

Demon Lover, Demon Lover,
What else can I do?
I have whispered awful things
Calling out to you.
I have made a waxen man
And bound it to my heart.
Burned the devil's candle—
Still you stay apart.

Demon Lover, Demon Lover,
What is this you say?
I must do these things at night,
Never by the day—
Only by the gibbous
Moon and the gallows tree
Can you find the pathway
Leading you to me.

Demon Lover, Demon Lover,
High the moon, and shrill
Croaks the lonely raven
On the gallows hill.
There's stirring in the marches,
But oh my heart is numb,
For now oh Demon Lover
At last, at last you come!

Weird Tales, November 1953

Siren Spotlight on Page Cooper

As I was researching the biographies of the women in this book, I assumed that I'd uncover some evidence that some of them were queer. All of these fiery, passionate women poets, many of whom never married . . . I mean, *come on.*

So I was extremely excited to see this tidbit in the *New York Herald Tribune*'s publishing-related gossip column "Turns with a Bookworm" in 1930: "Then we got lost on Long Island and stumbled onto the summer cottage of Page Cooper and Julie Brown, which hangs like an eyebrow on the cliff overlooking Glen Cove." (Brown was an illustrator whose work sometimes appeared in the *Herald Tribune.* A column the following year named her as someone who you could count on to help you carry bricks, whatever that means.) Two single ladies owning a Long Island vacation home together in the 1930s? Excited is an understatement—I sent Jaclyn a link to "Finally" by CeCe Penniston. Of course, we can't know for sure. But we know.

Anice Page Cooper (1891–1958) was born in West Virginia to a wealthy family (she was a regular in the society pages of the *Washington Post*) and entered New York's publishing world at some point in the 1920s. By 1930 she was working for Doubleday Doran, where she wrote ad copy for forthcoming books. She also wrote book reviews for the *Herald Tribune* and *Los Angeles Times.*

She was active in the city's publishing social scene, mentioned several times in "Turns with a Bookworm." She was also a prolific writer: Starting in the 1930s, she co-wrote celebrity biographies with people like Friedelind Wagner, granddaughter of the composer Richard Wagner. During World War II she served as a Naval correspondent covering military nurses, and her book *Navy Nurse* won the Navy Award. After the war she wrote fiction for younger readers, including many books about horses. She moved to Charleston, South Carolina, in the spring of 1957 and died there less than a year later.

Michael W. Phillips Jr.

They Burned a Witch in Bingham Square
Poems about Unruly Women

Horror is the genre to give us the competent, badass, don't-mess-with-me Final Girl, a trope that dates back at least to 1974, the year that brought us both *The Texas Chainsaw Massacre*'s Sally Hardesty and *Black Christmas*'s Jess Bradford.

But in classic horror, the damsels tend to lean less strong, more distressed, less don't-mess-with-me, more for-the-love-of-Christianity's-God-save-me-from-the-monster.

It's what makes some of the poems in this chapter extra special: These women don't need saving, and they're (mostly) not in distress. Because they're causing the distress. They are the distress. (Apologies to Pauline Booker. We wish the subject of your poem had had way more fun worshipping *at the shrine of painted flesh and pagan wine.*)

Even when they're expressing regret—*Sad I be, / Sad I be / When the changeling blood runs green in me*—they're also pretty stoked for all that green blood: Leah Bodine Drake's speaker in "Changeling" may be weepy, but she's happy and wise, too. (Changelings are the strange or deformed offspring of the fairies or elves, who leave their changelings in place of the human infant they've stolen.)

A number of the speakers and subjects in this chapter are thrilled to be the witches or the monsters, the causers-of-doom and bringers-of-pain. They lean into it, and they own it.

Consider Drake's "The Wood-Wife":

I've queer spells, potent spells
That I want to learn
To the goat-hooved and shaggy ones
Who hide in the fern.

This darling is straight up teaching classes for wood-wifery. (A wood wife, which comes from Germanic mythology, is a female forest spirit. They're gentle and beautiful, with wizened faces.)

I asked horror writer Paula D. Ashe for some insight into these stories of women behaving deliciously badly, and she pointed out that these poems—and horror in general, and, pulling back even more, the umbrella of literature—is a safe space for truth, for sharing what a person actually wants or thinks.

"Horror has always been a place for wild women," says Ashe, whose 2023 story collection *We Are Here to Hurt Each Other* won the Shirley Jackson Award and was nominated for a Bram Stoker Award. "It's always been a place where you can express the stuff that's not socially acceptable because you can just say, 'It's horror. I just made it up. It's fantasy. It's over-the-top. It's meant to be supernatural.' You can always put a little distance between yourself and what's happening in the work.

"Certainly for marginalized creators and writers and artists—whether they're women, whether they're queer, people of color—I think horror gives you a space. It also gives you a space to kind of attack the status quo."

The subject of Dorothy Quick's "Walpurgis Night" is a perfect example of this. The woman in her poem *loved the house and her own fireside*. Her man was dear and he held her tight but still, *She left his arms and the fireside's heat, / She left the joy of her own heart beat* for the voices calling to her outside the protective cocoon of all she was taught to want—*love and light and fire*—for what she actually wanted—*strange unknown desire*. She exercises her own agency and ditches a life of domesticity to answer the call of Walpurgis Night, a celebration that combines a spring pagan fertility party with the legend of St. Walburga, who was canonized on May 1. On Walpurgis Night, witches and devils are said to rollick in the Harz mountains to celebrate the arrival of spring.

Which apparently sounds like a pretty good time for a bored housewife looking for an evening with a little more punch.

Jaclyn Youhana Garver

Beware, of Vampire Women
Patricia Burgess

You must not wanton with each casual maiden,
Or the succubi may clasp you very soon.
Your heart is prodigal when roaming lightly—
Too easily distracted by the moon.
For when a siren seated by the wayside
May dazzle with an eloquent allure,
And melts your heart with diabolic beauty:
Such perilous adventure leaves no cure.

So cease your playing with the lotus damsels,
One never knows a demon in disguise;
Her voice is low and purring like a kitten;
Erotic, wax and wane her jacinth eyes.
Beware, you fickle cavalier of fortune;
You may be lost forever in an hour.
For a creature subtly warm, perversely human
May bleed your soul . . . silk-smiling to devour.

Weird Tales, July 1954

The Wood-Wife
Leah Bodine Drake

In a hollow oak-tree
    I live by the wood,
A bit more than human
    And much less than good.

I've queer spells, potent spells,
    That I want to learn
To the goat-hooved and shaggy ones
    Who hide in the fern.

The good-wives, the house-wives,
    They shudder at my sin:
But much they'd give to learn to weave
    Cloth of spiders'-spin!

My pet fox, my russet fox,
    He ravishes their geese:
Yet none dare call out the hounds
    If they would know peace!

On a day of falling leaves
    I met the young Squire.
I gave him a sidelong look
    That set his face afire.

The bonny young Squire,
    He dreams in a spell;
But not of golden curlylocks
    Of Parson Jones' Nell—
But of red hair, and green eyes
    That have looked on Hell!

Dream, pretty Squire-kin!
    It's small use to burn!
For when the moon is up
    The wood-wife will turn

Three times widdershins,
    And greet where you stood
The shagged-men, the satyr-men
    Who creep from the wood!

Weird Tales, March 1942

The Eldritch One
Pauline Booker

I've lived for long, uncounted eons,
    Since Time and I were young;
I dwell in crypts and hidden eyries,
    And speak with witch's tongue.

When blood drips from the horned moon,
    And wild winds lash the sea,
And men and ships die in the night,
    I laugh with demon-glee.

For well I know my evil curse—
    That I shall never die;
My soul will dwell in snakes and toads,
    And bats that blindly fly.

I walk my dark, forbidden ways,
    And none of human race
Can ever flee my awful spell,
    Who look upon my face.

And when at last the sun grows cold
    In its vain, ageless quest,
I'll seek once more the alien land
    Where I was born unblest.

Weird Tales, May 1948

The Hill Woman
Frances Elliott

The valley people wondered at her choice,
     The old house groping up the straggling hill,
With mold'ring walls that echoed back her voice
     And vistas that were always blank and still
As ancient dreams; they never really knew
     The hill flowers had such laughing Pixy eyes,
Hill clouds with silver pitchers poured the dew
     As dawn fans quivered in the orchid skies.

She hugged the secret of her wishing well,
     A whispering madness when the luring Junes
Tossed ragged roses in a drowsy spell
     That burgeoned to the bee's bass-violed tunes.
The valley people marvelled as their spires
     Caught up the splendor of her altar fires.

Weird Tales, October 1934

Inheritance
Sudie Stuart Hager

I'm grateful to people, a thousand years back,
Who let their minds run on a fanciful track—
Saw silver-winged fairies dance lightly in rain;
Heard witches conniving at trickery and pain;
Felt shivers when ogres, hobgoblins and gnomes
Shrieked nightly in forests or haunted their homes.

I, too, search for eggs Easter rabbits have laid,
And footprints where shy woodland brownies have played;
Deliciously shudder at Hallowe'en bats,
Great owls, with eyes flaming, and spitting, black cats.

Had all folk bequeathed things of practical need,
Oh, life would be prosy and meager indeed!

Weird Tales, July 1940

Changeling
Leah Bodine Drake

I am out on the wind
    In the wild, black night;
On the wings of the owl
    I take my flight,
On the ghostly wings of the great white owl;
And whether the night be fair or foul,
Or the moon be up or the thunder growl,
    Happy I be,
    Happy I be
When the changeling blood runs green in me!

When meek folks sleep
    In their dull, soft beds,
I creep over roots
    That the weasel treads,
Where the squat green lamps of the toadstools glow—
And only the fox knows the ways I go,
And nobody knows the things I know.
    Wise I be,
    Wise I be
When the changeling blood runs green in me!

O Mother, slumber
    And do not wake!
Thin voices called
    From the rain-wet brake,
And the child you cradled against your breast
Is out in the night on the black wind's crest,
For only the wild can give me rest.
    Sad I be,
    Sad I be
When the changeling blood runs green in me.

Weird Tales, September 1942

Requiem for a Sinner
Pauline Booker

Long you trod the twisted ways,
Through evil nights and haunted days;
And long you worshipped at the shrine
Of painted flesh and pagan wine,
Where harlots wore their shameful arts,
Unsheltered, on their facial charts;
And when the festive cup was drained,
The fiery brew had seared and stained
Your soul till it was claimed at last,
A forfeit to your crimson past.

Now deep within your tattered breast,
The embers of regret are burning,
As down the distant trails you go,
To demon-bournes past all returning.

Weird Tales, May 1953

Walpurgis Night
Dorothy Quick

She loved the house and her own fireside.
The hearth was dark and it stretches wide.

Her man was dear and he held her tight.
Outside were the calls of Walpurgis night.

She left his arms and the fireside's heat,
She left the joy of her own heart beat,

She opened the door and music came.
While a hundred voices called her name.

Within was love and light and fire.
Without was strange unknown desire.

The wind swirled in, the wind swirled out.
It whipped her long skirts all about.

She stepped outside, the door closed fast.
The voices whispered, "You've come at last!"

Strange hands caught her and pulled her on
When the door was opened—she was gone.

Weird Tales, January 1954

Heard on the Roof at Midnight
Leah Bodine Drake

As I sat by my fire one night
Witches I heard on the roof alight.
I heard their broomsticks whinny and neigh,
And then I heard one beldame say:

"Well met in darkness, Tess, my lass!
Have you seen our coven comrades pass?"
"Aye, Lib! The Kelpie from her tarn,
And half the cats from the miller's barn
Tore through the air with fiery eyes,
Each one grown to twice his size!
The hen-wife passed in a weasel's habit—
Oh, the coven gathers for the Sabbat!"

Then my blood ran cold, and hot again,
As I heard the witches (heard them plain),
Cry, "You who doze by the dullard hearth,
Open your soul to the ancient mirth!
Chain no longer your secret self;
Take down the besom from its shelf!
The owl's cried twice, the night wind moans,
The moon grins over the Sarsen Stones,
Fling wide the casement, mount and ride—
Walpurgis Night is all outside!"

Then I barred my window, I said a prayer;
(To listen longer I didn't dare!)
I clasped the Book and I closed my eyes. . . .
I heard them rush through the midnight skies!
So I looked out the window: all was bare,
Roof and ridgepole and milky air,
And only two bats, who vanished soon,
Were winging their way across the moon.

Weird Tales, November 1946

Witch-Burning
Mary Elizabeth Counselman

They burned a witch in Bingham Square
    Last Friday afternoon.
The faggot-smoke was blacker than
    The shadows on the moon;
The licking flames were strangely green
    Like fox-fire on the fen . . .
And she who cursed the godly folk
    Will never curse again.

They burned a witch in Bingham Square
    Before the village gate.
A huswife raised a skinny hand
    To damn her, tense with hate.
A huckster threw a jagged stone—
    Her pallid cheek ran red . . .
But there was something scornful in
    The way she held her head.

They burned a witch in Bingham Square;
    Her eyes were terror-wild.
She was a slight, a comely maid,
    No taller than a child.
They bound her fast against the stake
    And laughed to see her fear . . .
Her red lips muttered secret words
    That no one dared to hear.

They burned a witch in Bingham Square—
    But ere she swooned with pain
And ere her bones were sodden ash
    Beneath the sudden rain,
She set her mark upon that throng . . .
    For time cannot erase
The echo of her anguished cries,
    The memory of her face.

Weird Tales, October 1936

Siren Spotlight on Pauline Booker

Pauline Booker (1913–1967) was a lifelong resident of Texas. Between 1941 and 1955, she published dozens of poems in romance magazines such as *Love Book Magazine* and romantic western magazines (which were an actual thing) like *Rangeland Romances*, in addition to selling three poems to *Weird Tales*. She also wrote articles about fashion and Native American history.

While researching this book, I found a small window into Booker's personality in the form of a July 1948 letter to *Writers Digest*. It helped me flesh out her biography a bit—she name-drops the editors of several of the romance magazines she published with, so I knew I had the right Pauline Booker. She signed the letter "Pauline Booker, Goldthwaite, TX," which allowed me to find her birth and death dates via her gravestone.

But the letter also gives a glimpse of a playful, flirtatious woman who enjoys the life of a poet. "I like the pictures of men . . . you use on the cover. You see, I'm a single gal and frankly admit I like a picture of a youngish and handsome male any time." She singles out *Weird Tales* associate editor Lamont Buchanan, calling him "my favorite editor" and wondering if he's "youngish and good-looking? If so, I'd like to see a pix of him sometime. He writes mighty nice letters!" (Editor's note: Buchanan married his childhood sweetheart in 1948.)

Michael W. Phillips Jr.

Evil Things That Haven't Any Name
Poems of Supernatural Creatures

I am an atrocious housekeeper. My home is not dirty, but cluttered. There are usually some dishes in the sink. There are some piles of clothes in my closet that I need to bag up and get to Goodwill. I work from home, and my "office chair" is our couch. I'm on it right now. My "desk" is the coffee table in front of me. On it, I spy a long-necked lighter I use to reach inside low candles, a stack of notecards, a hair clip, some earrings, my journal, lip balm.

My mother, by comparison, is a brilliant housekeeper. Everything is always in its place. There is never dust on anything. Goodwill (or is it AMVETS?) drops by every six weeks to pick up the piles of clothes she never lets accumulate on the closet floor.

Keeping things tidy is a way she shows love. Ensuring those in the house are comfortable? It's how she says "I love you." The six-ish pillows on the guestroom bed—actual pillows you could sleep on, we're not even getting into the decorative ones—are an act of love, allowing my spouse and me to pick a flat or fluffy, down or synthetic pillow to our liking when we visit.

Even though it's not one of the ways I best show my love for others, I recognize "I care for you and wish to ensure your comfort" as a way many others do show their love—and it's one I hear loudly, perhaps because I've seen it in my mother all my life.

I think this is why I'm so affected by Louise Garwood's "Ghost." While vampires, werewolves, monsters, and all sorts of ghosts and specters haunt this chapter, I could argue that the most horrifying poem in this section—hell, in this book—is this little poem, told by a ghost worrying about the love she left behind, wondering who'll take care of her *dear heart . . . now that you are alone!*

It's not terribly substantial in terms of the amount of content. Its eight lines split into two stanzas certainly can't fight the 23 four-line stanzas in "The Ballad of the Jabberwock." "Ghost" doesn't do anything fancy with its verbiage, uses a simple aa, bb, cc, dd rhyme scheme. But its sentiment and the grief of its narrator haunt me. I think I've read this poem more than any other in this collection because it's so full of sadness, you can feel the narrator's woe under your skin and in your gums. Why can't this ghost move on? Does her love tether her to the one she left behind? Did she take care of this person because she loved them romantically, as I like to assume? Or is the one she left behind a child? The person she's speaking to, were they a parent, perhaps, or a patient? Was she a caretaker for someone who could not live alone because of physical or mental disability?

Perhaps the power of this poem lies in the ambiguity, letting readers bring their own assumptions and experiences to the verse.

There is great fun to be found in monsters and ghosts, in Leah Bodine Drake's werewolves *who have forgotten the speech of men, making Good people on their house-doors mark / A cross, and hug their hearths in fright*, and her jabberwock who was

> Horned like a billy-goat
> And scaled like a dragon,
> Perched cross-legged on
> Their brand-new wagon.

But I can't imagine a worse horror than to find yourself gone from this life and unable to move on to whatever comes next because you can't let go of the love you left behind.

Jaclyn Youhana Garver

Moon Phantoms
Dorothy Haynes Madlé

The years are hungry hounds that run and bay
    Upon the spoor of our slow-paced delight;
Awhile we hold them with the lifted lash
    Of laughter—but the moon is low tonight.

The moon behind us is a golden club
    Driving ahead the shadows of the years;
They overtake ours, dark upon the grass
    —Swift are the moon-cast phantoms, swift the fears.

Have you a morsel to cast back, to set
    The time-hounds from our traces? See, I fling
Before their avid jaws by little store
    Of garnered necromancy, and you sing
A brave, high melody, and they are still.
    What is that other shadow, walking vast
Toward us? As it strides the sloping hill
    Its hands hold looped grey leashes, and the pack
Runs silent to its heel. Where is the moon?
Where are the yapping shadows—and our own?

Weird Tales, July 1946

They Run Again

Leah Bodine Drake

Beyond the black and naked wood
    In frosty gold has set the sun,
And dusk glides forth in cobweb hood. . . .
    Sister, tonight the werewolves run!

With white teeth gleaming and eyes aflame
    The werewolves gather upon the howe!
Country churl and village dame,
    They have forgotten the wheel and plow.

They have forgotten the speech of men;
    Their throats are dry with a dreadful thirst;
And woe to the traveler in the glen
    Who meets tonight with that band accurst!

Now from the hollows creeps the dark;
    The moon like a yellow owl takes flight;
Good people on their house-doors mark
    A cross, and hug their hearths in fright.

Sister, listen! . . . The King-Wolf howls!
    The pack is running! . . . Drink down the brew,
Don the unearthly, shaggy cowls—
    We must be running, too!

Weird Tales, June-July 1939

Vampires
Dorothy Quick

The old books tell of how the werewolf came
With white fangs gleaming redly in the night,
Of evil things that haven't any name,
That cannot bear the searching rays of light.
They tell of unknown horrors, deadly deeds;
Of vampires, who can leave their coffin bed
And fly abroad to satisfy their needs
With human blood. So age-old books have said.

There still are vampires walking on our ways,
Not creatures from the grave, but men who live
On someone else's heart's blood all their days,
Men who take all they can but never give;
Strange men who ever striving for their goals
Achieve their way by crushing human souls.

Weird Tales, September 1935

The Ballad of the Jabberwock
A True Tale of Squankom[1] Town
Leah Bodine Drake

My grandmother tells me,
    When the lights are low,
How the Jabberwock appeared
    In Squankom, long ago.

First a frightened farmer,
    Tearing into town,
Told how his wife had seen
    Something big and brown,

Horned like a billy-goat
    And scaled like a dragon,
Perched cross-legged on
    Their brand-new wagon.

It leaped into the barn
    And hid in the hay.
She screeched bloody murder
    And fainted away!

The Timmermans saw it,
    Coming from Cross Keys;
It crept through Corkray's Wood
    And peered 'round the trees.

Footprints were found in fields
    Clawed like a bird's;
It clumped over Marsh's roof,
    Gibbering words.

The folks began to see It
    Here and everywhere,
Clinging to the steeple,
    Winging through the air

With vans of mighty bat;
    Or walking in a pasture
Upright as any man,
    And cocky as a master!

Squankom locked all its doors,
    And bright lamps were lit
In chilly front parlors
    Where folks seldom sit

Except for a funeral,
    Or a minister's call.
But what lurks in darkness?
    They lighted up all.

Some few were skeptical
    And would only smile;
But the path to the barn at night
    Seemed like a mile!

Reverend Walsey preached of sin,
    And most folks agreed
That It was a warning
    They had better heed.

They named It *The Jabberwock*
    For want of another;
But some shook their heads: "It's
    The Devil's own brother!"

The people came to church
    Who'd never been yet.
Some patched up a quarrel,
    And some paid a debt.

Cousin Jo and Cousin Kate
    Forgot they didn't speak;
And Old Man Jones stayed sober
    For one amazing week.

Wives left off nagging,
    And husbands kissed their wives.
The Claybrook brothers went to work
    For once in their lives.

No one watered any milk
    Or cut the measures down;
And Tillie got religion
    And all her girls left town!

Then one day the town awoke
    To find It had fled;
No one saw it squatting
    On his barn or shed.

No one saw those footprints
    Huge upon his lawn . . .
Suddenly, as it had come,
    The Jabberwock had gone.

The church held a meeting
    And great thanks were given
That Satan had done his worst
    And left them scared but shriven.

Satan had romped about
    Like a roaring lion;
But Squankom held firm, and now
    Was a little Zion.

They were the wonder-town
    Of the countryside!
They had driven Evil out!
    They let good abide.

For almost a fortnight . . .
    Then someone stole a sack
Of flour out of Barker's store,
    And Tillie's girls came back.

Dark of the Moon anthology

Disillusionment
Victoria Beaudin Johnson

Slow moving, from the tomb of years,
    Unbidden shadows come to me;
I greet them with a hollow voice,
    Nor hide the tears that they must see.

We muse on all that might have been;
    Too well we know how strange it seems
That Age, the ghost of yesterday,
    Communes with shades of perished dreams.

You who have faith and youth and love,
    Can not discern this spectral host;
Too dazed with hope you can not see
    These shadows talking to a ghost.

Weird Tales, December 1935

The Singing Shadow
Yetza Gillespie

Nobody came through the moonlight,
Nobody knocked on the door,
Singing, by way of a greeting,
An old light-hearted score;

But a shadow crossed the moonpath
And leaned against the door,
And something sang from the darkness,
That elsewhere sings no more.

Weird Tales, September 1952

Ghosts

Louise Garwood

Who tapped upon my window pane
And sighed and laughed and sighed again,
    Till I called aloud so the stillness heard
    A sweet, a long-unspoken word?
Was it only wind and rain?

Yesterday, with whisper slight,
Footfalls followed me, quick and light,
    Fluttering, restless close behind:
    Who went where my garden pathways wind?
Dry leaves of crimson bright?

Who wails my name with sobbing cry
So that I wake and weeping lie?
    A string of the violoncello broke,
    In its dusty case—but yet—who spoke?
Who sighs? Who passes by?

Weird Tales, July 1926

Listening
Cristel Hastings

The night seems to be listening
To furtive little sounds—
To halting footsteps of a ghost
That makes its stealthy rounds
Seeking the names that once it knew
That now are carved on stone
And granite shafts that etch a hill
Where grieving night winds moan.

The night seems to be listening
For voices it once knew
And loved, and carried tenderly
Through vaults of midnight blue.
A moonbeam sifts through somber pines
Whose shadows make dim caves—
A ghostly light moves softly on
Among the silent graves.

The night is listening—the wind
Goes sobbing down the years—
Dawn lights the slender shafts with dew
But Night knows they are tears.

Weird Tales, February 1935

The Dead Speak
Vivian Stratton

Last night I saw you standing by my bier
    In lonely, broken-hearted agony.
I spoke to you, but could not make you hear,
    I stood beside you, but you did not see.
I stroked your hair when you were on your knees
In prayer; you felt, but thought it was a breeze.

Despairingly, I whispered in your ear:
    You thought it was the beating of your heart.
The time was short for me to linger here,
    God's voice had called, and so I must depart.
One candle flared into a tall, black plume
As wearily I sighed and left the room.

Weird Tales, October 1939

Ghost

Louise Garwood

Your shoes are muddy . . . you'll not track the floor?
Nor fail to double-latch and try the door?
    The kitchen window—have you made it fast?
    Now put the screen around the fireplace, last.

Before you go upstairs—that pantry light—
You know it used to burn, sometimes, all night.
    To bed, dear heart! How thoughtful you have grown
    Of little tasks, now that you are alone!

Weird Tales, December 1931

Return

Leona May Ames

I shall return a lonely little ghost,
    And creep into your arms some cloudy night.
You shall not know me, save that in your heart
    Old pain shall stir, and quick tears blur your sight.

You shall have no way then of knowing me,
    Save, when a bitter little wind shall moan,
You shall be suddenly aware that life
    Is cold and wide, and you are all alone.

Weird Tales, November 1931

Weird Things
Vivian Stratton

The weirdest things have happened since he died.
A phantom hound sat on the porch and cried;
And scent of moldy earth is on the breeze,
While shapeless *things* at night flit through the trees!
The water pipes sweat drops of bloody red,
As ghostly footsteps fall with measured tread,
And basement lights grow dim, while at the door
Come clawing noises, never heard before!
Gigantic shadows flicker on the wall
When candles flare to smoke-plumes, black and tall;
And curtains wave when not a breath of air
Is stirring, eery noise is everywhere!
He was so kind, I know it can't be he
Who does these things, but, oh, what *can* it be!

Weird Tales, December 1939

Siren Spotlight on Louise Garwood

Between 1925 and 1931, a woman named Louis Garwood published two stories and three poems in *Weird Tales*, plus one poem in a romance magazine. That's all anyone knows about her for certain, but I did some digging and some informed speculation. Since this is a book of speculative poetry, I trust that you'll bear with me.

From the February 1924 issue of *Poetry Magazine*, I learned that the Poetry Society of Texas gave an award to a woman named Louise Garwood. I got in touch with the Poetry Society, but their historian was unable to provide me with info other than the award and the fact that Garwood lived in Houston's Montrose neighborhood.

Judge Hiram Garwood, a Texas state representative and president of the Texas State Bar Association, lived in Montrose with his daughter Louise. The Garwoods were a prominent enough family that the social gossip column of the *Houston Post* mentioned Louise's attendance at various parties in 1925. Around the same time, a Texan named Louise Garwood wrote lyrics to a song called "Rainbow Tears" with music by Wilson Fraser, and someone named Louise Garwood sent the lyrics of a Texas blues song to Dorothy Scarborough for her book *On the Trail of Negro Folk-Songs* in 1925. Could they be the same woman?

From there, the trail goes cold until 1957, when Miss Louise Garwood became a member of the South Texas Historical Association.[2] Her address was listed as Sheppard Pratt Hospital outside of Baltimore, Maryland. A Google search produced a social worker living in the same town with the middle and last name Louise Garwood. Maybe a daughter or granddaughter? I got in touch. No relation, but the woman informed me that Sheppard Pratt was a swanky private psychiatric hospital—the kind of place a prominent Texas lawyer might send his daughter.

When this Louise Garwood died in 1980, Brigadier General Maurice

Hirsch made a gift in her honor to the Rice University Library. She was buried in Texas with her family.[3]

Was it the same woman? I can't know for sure. But it feels right.

Michael W. Phillips Jr.

Notes

1. Squankom (usually Squankum, though we're keeping Drake's spelling), from a Lenape word meaning "a place where evil spirits dwell," was the name of the south Jersey village of Williamstown, one of the places where the mysterious creature variously called the "Jersey Devil" or "Jabberwock" was seen around the turn of the century. "The Ballad of the Jabberwock" won first prize in the 1946 Stephen Vincent Benet Ballad Contest, held annually by the Word Weavers.
2. *Southwestern Historical Quarterly*, April 1957.
3. Rice University *Flyleaf*, Summer 1980.

There Is a Sighing Sound in Every Room
Haunted House Poems

Man, I love a haunted house.

And while Mike and I pored through a couple hundred vintage horror poems to put together this collection, one particular subgenre jumped out as a favorite among the poems under consideration: the haunted house poem.

Now, did they start to sound repetitive? Yes. Did we laugh at the fact that so many of the titles mirrored each other, at the poets' utter refusal to grab a thesaurus or get a little thoughtful with their titles? Also yes. Did we ache for a new turn of phrase, an unexpected narrator, a punchline to knock us out? We sure did.

Did we find standouts?

Absolutely.

The following poems deal with your traditional haunted house accoutrements: *old doors / (that) Move back and forth propelled by unseen hands / On hinges long unused; Sudden drafts that seem like breaths, / And a fluttering of bats; a sighing sound in every room.* But there is, too, an unexpected amount of space given to the stairs, that site of tiptoed creeps to inspect an aforementioned sigh, perhaps, or surveying a staircase to nowhere. There are the lonely ghosts, who miss a beloved. Murderous ghosts, who are stuck at the scene of the crime. Noisy ghosts, who moan, laugh, and cry.

The supernatural subset is my favorite genre of horror, and haunted houses may well be one of the most popular in a favorite category. And why not? I've never been at sea, fearful of the finger-shaped wisps of mist curling around my ship's mast, nor have I stood on a shore, scanning the horizon for the boat that carried away my lover, leaving me sad and unsure if he'd been capsized or captured. I've never met a vampire or worried that I or someone I love is possessed by a demon.

But I have wondered why my house was making so many damn noises when I was the only one home. I have tucked my toes beneath the covers to avoid tempting the under-the-bed ghosts that I don't even believe in. And I've gotten up in the middle of the night to use the restroom and refused to look into the mirror because...what if?

Your brain might know there is no Something lurking in the hall, flickering a blue light, humming a haunted lullaby, and waiting for you to fall asleep so she can trace a cold fingertip along your soft cheek, leach a sweet little fraction of your warmth.

But tell that to the gooseflesh on your arms.

Jaclyn Youhana Garver

An Empty House at Night
Cristel Hastings

Quiet enough at noon among its trees
    And weed-grown paths that slumber in the sun,
The empty house seems settled back at ease
    Watching the gray years drift by, one by one.

Here bees may drone and plunder at their will
    In gardens long forgotten—here a bird
May twitter under eaves where all is still
    And somnolent—where never voice is heard.

But let night come!—the old house is *alive*
    With sound and motion with each wind that sighs!
An empty house at night becomes a hive
    Of creeping monsters with a thousand eyes.

Each leaf that falls is like a giant's stride
    Across a roof velvet with moss and mold—
Here settling timbers creak—here dragons hide
    To slither from their attics, queerly bold.

The empty rooms are peopled in the gloom
    With hordes of shapeless, voiceless ghosts that roam
Through doors and windows and from room to room
    Of this lone place that once was known as Home.

Winds weep and wail the long nights through—old doors
    Move back and forth propelled by unseen hands
On hinges long unused—along the floors
    Sly forms may stalk the boards in fearsome bands.

Huge spiders spin their curtains, gray and wide,
    On grimy windows shutting out the light
For fear some passer-by may see inside
    The ghostly things that haunt the place at night.

Weird Tales, April 1935

Haunted Mansion
Marietta Hawley

It stands alone on a haunted shore,
With curious words of a deathless lore
    On its massive gate empearled;
And its carefully guarded, mystic key
Hideth its solemn mystery
    From the seeking eyes of the world.

And pictures out of each haunted room
Up through the ghostly shadows loom
    And gleam with a spectral light;
Pictures lit with a radiant glow,
And some that image such desolate wo
    That weeping you turn from the sight.

And oft do its stately walls repeat
Echoes of music wildly sweet,
    Swelling to gladness high;
With mournful ballads of ancient time,
And funeral hymns—and a nursery rime,
    Dying away in a sigh.

And oft in the silence of midnight air
You hear on its stately winding-stair
    The echoes of fairy feet;
Gentle footsteps, that lightly fall
Through the enchanted castle-hall
    And up in the golden street.

And still in a dark, forsaken tower,
Crowned with a withered cypress-flower,
    Is a bowed head turned away;
A face like carvèd marble white,
Sweet eyes drooping away from the light,
    Shunning the eye of day.

Mysteries strange its still walls keep;
Strange are the crowds that through it sweep,
    Walking by night and day;
But evermore will the castle-hall
Echo their footsteps' phantom fall,
    Till its walls shall crumble away.

Weird Tales, November 1927

Steps in the Field
Leah Bodine Drake

In a field that no one weeds
A flight of stone steps upward leads
From the grass and Queen-Anne's-Lace:
It is a still and lonely pace.

There is no house there any more;
The steps go mounting to no door.
They lead the way but to the sky
Where the hawks are hovering high.

If trespassers climbed that stair
What would happen to them there?
Would they merely stand, and see
Where the portals used to be?

Maybe when they reached the top
They would find they could not stop—
Go on climbing, foot and shoe,
Secret stairways in the blue!

They might vanish, boot or dress,
Into sunny emptiness,
Leaving field and Queen-Anne's-Lace
For some very different place.

Though we know it's but a game
Children play there, just the same
Do not venture—what if you
Climbed those steps and found it true?

Weird Tales, November 1947

The Haunted Stairs
Yetza Gillespie

The staircase narrow as the way
Unto salvation's door,
Leads from a hall as dark as sin
With deep stains on the floor.

Nobody knows who climbed halfway
To where the turn is black,
What clutching fingers waited there
Who felt the heartstrings crack.

And no one knows what now ascends
The thirteenth step—and stops,
And flutters like a netted bird
Before it moans, and drops....

I'll step into the hall some night
When I forget my prayers,
And to my sorrow, see what stands
Upon the dreadful stairs.

Weird Tales, May 1946

In the Shadows
Leah Bodine Drake

As we went up the narrow stair,
    My candle slim and I,
From the crouching shadows came
    A little tired sigh.

And there was nothing on the stair
    Or in my garret room,
But cobwebs on the rafters,
    And corners filled with gloom.

And still and silent was the house,
    And dark and still the air. . . .
But where the shadows wavered
    In the candle-flare,
Something small, unearthly, sighed
    Out of some strange despair.

Weird Tales, October 1935

An Old House

Cristel Hastings

Bathed in mystery and moonlight,
    Wistfully it stands
At the end of a lonely, winding road
    Where cobwebs hang in strands
Of dusty lace an old ghost hung
    Before a sagging door—
And winds go moaning through the rooms
    With fog from down the moor.

Never a light—nor sound, nor laugh—
    Never a footfall—wait!
What was that?—did I hear a step
    Down by the creaking gate?
Echoes resounding in empty halls—
    Shadows that spring like cats—
Sudden drafts that seem like breaths,
    And a fluttering of bats.

Eery tenants—ghosts of old—
    Loves and griefs—and tears—
Underneath a leaking roof
    Haunting mildewed years.
Straggling roses climb the porches
    Hiding broken panes,
Though their roots be dry and fainting
    Waiting for the rains.

Bathed in silent, moonlit fragrance,
    I hear the old ghosts talk—
Must be wind in that old maple
    Down the lonely walk.
Bats, and broken, paneless windows—
    Creaking shutters—weeds—
Loneliness and sobbing wind ghosts,
    Wait for the friend it needs.

Weird Tales, November 1927

The Haunted Castle

Lilla Price Savino

Pale ghosts, with snowy hands and flowing hair,
    Are gliding up and down yon stairs and hall;
Tall shapes, in armor clad or fabrics rare,
    Hasten in answer to their loved ones' call.

For this old castle, standing on a hill,
    Has seen twelve generations rise and fall,
And now the last man of its line lies still
    Within the churchyard, near the crumbling wall.

And yet, within its spacious halls and rooms,
    A troop of merrymakers holds full sway—
Spirits of those who here held happy court
    In wondrous glory of a bygone day.

Mortals who pass see lights and hear strange sounds
    And flee in terror from the fearful place;
They say the castle's haunted by the dead
    Of that ancestral line of noble race.

Play on, pale ghosts, until the cold, gray dawn
    Warns you to seek again your narrow beds,
And, in your tattered grandeur, sink to rest
    Beneath the crumbling stones that mark your heads.

Weird Tales, April 1928

Deserted House
Marion Doyle

I thought:
Here are but echoing emptiness and dust,
Silence and mystery, dead dreams of old desires;
But over the foot-marred threshold shadows thrust
Their fingers, groping for the phantom fires
Of a pale moon's light that lies like sunlight spent
Upon the tangled grasses of the lawn;
Here are faint, half-heard whispers, eloquent
Of vanished voices; the phenomenon
Of printless footfalls; on the rotted rafter,
Perched like storm-driven and bewildered birds,
Flutter the shades of long-lost tears and laughter,
Of ruffled, smooth, of gray and irised words:

Hearing the echoed cries of birth and death,
Hearing the muted whisper of old vows,
There is a Something catches at the breath;
Something defies the name—Deserted House.

Weird Tales, September 1933

The Haunted Room

Cristel Hastings

What is it that goes creeping through this room,
    Trailing its dusty garments as it crawls?
Why does the air seem like an icy breath
    That penetrates the dim and empty halls?

They say that Death came once into this room—
    That old four-poster in the corner there—
They whisper, too, of shrieks that pierce the night,
    Of banging doors, and blue light everywhere.

A rose that hung outside the shuttered pane
    Withered and died one night when shrill winds moaned—
The queer blue light hovered a while, and then
    The very timbers of the old house groaned.

Weeds now run riot in the somber path
    Like snares for careless feet that wander through,
But no one comes, for no one ventures near—
    Always there is the dim light, pale and blue.

The low winds moan even on summer nights—
    There is a sighing sound in every room.
The mice have full possession of the halls
    And hold their ghostly dance in shadowed gloom.

They say each night when sane folk's clocks strike twelve
    The blue light glows a while through shuttered panes,
And then it is the Thing comes crawling back
    And tries to rid the floor of crimson stains.

Weird Tales, August 1932

The Tenants
Leah Bodine Drake

Among the black trees spider-webbed
    Against a red and wintry dusk,
I leaned upon the sagging gate
    And looked up at the evil husk

Of that old house, remote from town
    And haunted, so the farm-folk said,
By brother-ghosts—the victim stabbed,
    The killer hanged 'til he was dead.

"How does it feel," I asked the pair
    Of farmers lounging in the door,
"To live within a haunted house?
    You must have nerves of steel and more!"

A hoot-owl cried within the wood;
    The sky above was red as sin;
The shadows deepened; side by side,
    Each figure eyed me with a grin.

Then one replied, "We have to stay—
    This is our home, the land we tilled—
For I'm the one they hanged," he said,
    "And he's the one I killed."

Dark of the Moon anthology

Siren Spotlight on Cristel Hastings

In addition to writing poetry, the women in this collection held day jobs: They were editors, journalists, bookstore managers, even a deputy sheriff. Many were probably housewives; many probably worked in unremarked jobs, helping to make ends meet.

Cristel Hastings (1888–1966) was the Secretary to the Chief Clerk of the California state legislature, where she worked six days a week and made $5 per day. She worked hard, and her employers appreciated her. There's an entry in the 1937 edition of the legislature's official record honoring her:

> Resolved: That the Assembly this day honors Miss Cristel Hastings, its efficient and charming Secretary to the Chief Clerk, and in this manner pays its homage to her in recognition of her great contributions in the field of literature; and be it further resolved, that the Assembly hereby encourages Miss Hastings in her chosen field and directs that her poem "Ship Models" be printed in this day's Journal.

She published more than 200 poems and short stories in romance magazines, western magazines, western romance magazines, and many others. Her seventeen poems in *Weird Tales* ties her for sixth-most poems in the magazine. She also wrote *Alta California: A Story of the Golden West in Rhyme*, an epic poem about the history of California. How did she find the time?

And then, in 1940, she stopped publishing poetry. Although she lived until 1966, there's no record of any publications during the last 26 years of her life. Did she retire? Did she suffer from an illness that kept her from writing? Did she decide that, rather than writing about her beloved California wilds, she'd rather experience them? There's a tree named after her in Humboldt Redwoods State Park in California. Maybe there's a clue there.

Michael W. Phillips Jr.

Poet Biographies

Birth and death dates are listed where available.

Rita Barr was a pseudonym used by Sara Borschow Bormaster (1910–2003), a poet, deputy sheriff, songwriter, and political activist from Texas. She published dozens of poems in national magazines and won several awards.[1]

Pauline Booker. See page 126.

Harriet A. Bradfield. See page 86.

Hazel Burden might have been Hazel Heltsley (née Burden), who was born in 1913 in Iowa, married Hugh Heltsley in 1938 (four years after the *Weird Tales* poem appeared), died in 2000 in Colorado, and "enjoyed reading and writing poetry and short stories," according to her obituary.[2]

Patricia Burgess. The poem included here is the only publication we can find, although search results are muddied by the existence of a more recent poet with the same name.

Brooke Byrne published the poem "Sic Transit Gloria" and a story called "The Werewolf's Howl" in *Weird Tales*. She could be the Elizabeth Brooke Byrne who served as the editor of the *Classical High School Gazette* in Lynn, Massachusetts, and, in 1932, won a $5 prize in a *Scholastic* poetry contest. That Byrne was sent to radio school as a second lieutenant in the Civilian Defense during World War II, where she became one of the first women to obtain a radio engineer's license. She returned to Lynn after the war and worked at the library, where she specialized in mending library books and published a book, *Mending Books Is Fun*, in 1957.[3]

M. Ludington Cain. See page 37.

Enola Chamberlain (1894-1976), also published as Chamberlin, was the daughter of pioneers who traveled from Iowa to California in a covered wagon in 1898. Much of her work appeared in publications associated with the Church of Jesus Christ of Latter-day Saints.[4]

Page Cooper. See page 111.

Mary Elizabeth Counselman (1911-1995) was one of the most prolific authors to appear in pulp magazines. Over the course of her career, which spanned more than sixty years, she contributed more than one hundred stories, poems, and articles to magazines including *Weird Tales*, *The Saturday Evening Post*, and *Good Housekeeping*.[5]

Marion Stauffer Doyle (1898-1974) was known as "the poet laureate of Somerset County" in Pennsylvania. In addition to the six poems she published in *Weird Tales* between 1932 and 1939, she published more than two thousand poems, articles, and stories in venues including the *New York Times*, *Chicago Tribune*, *McCall's*, *Saturday Evening Post*, and *Good Housekeeping*.[6]

Leah Bodine Drake. See page 24.

Frances Elliott published more than twenty poems in magazines including *Weird Tales*, *All-Story Love Stories*, and *Top-Notch Stories*.

Louise Garwood. See page 143.

Yetza Gillespie (1900-1964). In addition to the six poems she published in *Weird Tales*, Gillespie was incredibly prolific, in some years selling upward of 100 poems to various outlets including the *Saturday Evening Post* and *New York Times*. She managed a bookstore in Kansas City, Missouri, and took yearly vacations to South and Central America.[7]

Dorothy Gold. Aside from the single poem she published in *Weird Tales*, nothing is known about her.

Julia Boynton Green (1861-1957) had already published three volumes of poetry when, at the age of 70, she started writing sci-fi poems for pulp magazines. Born in New York, she lived much of her life in Redlands, California, on an orange farm with her husband, author Levi Worthington Green.[8]

Sudie Stuart Hager (1895-1982) was a teacher and poet who lived most of her life in Idaho, where she was the poet laureate from 1949 until her death. In addition to her poem in *Weird Tales*, she published poetry in the *Saturday Evening Post, Farm Journal*, and other outlets.[9]

Cristel Hastings. See page 158.

Marietta Hawley (1836-1926) was one of the most popular American authors of the nineteenth century, publishing more than two dozen books as "Josiah Allen's Wife." They're virtually forgotten now, but one of your editors read one of her books. Her "Samantha" series is about a rural woman who visits "exotic" places like Chicago and comments on them in her homespun style, and one of them is about the 1893 World's Columbian Exposition that produced the Ferris Wheel and H.H. Holmes, America's earliest known serial killer. The poem included here was originally published in 1867 and was reprinted in *Weird Tales* a year after she died.[10]

Sara Henderson Hay (1906-1987) was a prolific and award-winning poet who published six collections of poetry, one of which won the Edna St. Vincent Millay Award from the Poetry Society of America. She worked at the publishing company Charles Scribner's Sons and was married to composer Nikolai Lopatnikoff.[11]

Marjorie Holmes (1910-2002) was a best-selling Christian author and advice columnist whose critically maligned but immensely popular books included the *Two from Galilee* trilogy about the life of Jesus. She wrote articles and advice columns for the *Washington Evening Star, Reader's Digest, McCall's*, and more.[12]

Alice I'Anson (1872-1931) published five poems in *Weird Tales*, along with several in other outlets including *Oriental Stories, California Illustrated*, and *Overland Monthly*. She died in Mexico City in June 1931, and much of her work appeared posthumously.[13]

Minna Irving (1864-1940) was a pseudonym used by poet, songwriter, and journalist Minnie Odell. Between 1880 and 1937, she published far too many stories and poems to count, in outlets ranging from *Peterson's Magazine* (one of the most popular women's magazines of the nineteenth century) to *Weird Tales* (her last publication before her death).[14]

Leona Ames Hill (1904-1977). In addition to the poem she sold to *Weird Tales*, Hill published almost two dozen poems in outlets including the *New York Times*, *Washington Post*, and *American Mercury*. Late in life, she published two poetry collections. She and her husband owned an apple orchard in Michigan.[15]

Thelma E. Johnson. In addition to the poem in this book, Johnson published a story called "David Keeps His Word" in *Ghost Stories* in 1929. Stories in that magazine were presented as true, first-person accounts of encounters with ghosts (although most were written by staff writers). So maybe, based on "David Keeps His Word," Johnson "traveled about the country with (her) father's carnival and medicine show" as a child.

Victoria Beaudin Johnson (1899-1976) was a Midwestern poet who was born in Wisconsin and moved to the Detroit area in the 1930s. She received her master's degree from the University of Detroit and taught English at Highland Park High School. In addition to the poem included in this book, her poetry appeared in newspapers and *The English Journal*.[16]

Minnie Faegre Knox (1886-1980) was a poet and playwright who was active in the San Francisco Bay poetry and social scenes, serving as editor for the California Writers' Club and a member of the College Women's Club of Berkeley.[17]

Marie W. Linné. Aside from the poem that appears in this book, we could find no information about Linné.

Lilith Lorraine. See page 54.

Dorothy Haynes Madlé (1917-1980). In addition to the poem in this volume, Madlé (later credited as Madlee) published two short stories in *Fantastic Universe* and co-wrote the "Star Ka'at" series with Andre Norton.

Maisie Nelson. Aside from the poem in this volume, we were unable to find any information about Nelson. There was a Canadian poet named Maisie Nelson Devitt writing around the same time, but she was publishing as Devitt at least two years before Nelson's poem appeared, so it's unlikely that the two were the same person.

Edith Ogutsch (1929-1990) was born in Germany to a Jewish family. She was sent to London during World War II as part of the Kinder-transport, and her father died in the Theresienstadt concentration camp. Ogutsch was active in sci-fi fandom, publishing dozens of poems in fanzines and mainstream outlets including the *New Yorker* and the *Saturday Evening Post*.[18]

Dorothy Marie Peterkin was probably Dorothy M. Johnson (1905–1984), the woman who wrote the stories that became the classic Western films *The Man Who Shot Liberty Valance* and *A Man Called Horse*. Johnson was married briefly to a soldier named Peterkin, and in 1927 she published a story under the name Dorothy M. Johnson Peterkin. After her divorce, Johnson became famous under her maiden name.[19]

Lilla Pool Price (1848-1914) was a music teacher, composer, and poet from North Carolina. She published several poems in *Peterson's Magazine*, a popular women's magazine of the late 19th century. Her poem "A Grave" was originally printed there. Her daughter, Lilla Price Savino, also has a poem in this book.[20]

Nina Wilcox Putnam (1888-1962) was incredibly prolific, publishing several books, more than 500 stories, and thousands of articles. At least a dozen of her stories were adapted into films, most famously *The Mummy* (1932).[21]

June Power Reilly (1885-1973) published one poem in *Weird Tales*. She was descended from a Revolutionary War soldier. Abraham Lincoln argued his first case at a courthouse on her grandfather's farm, and her uncle was the judge who presided over Lincoln's last case before Lincoln was elected president.[22]

Lucrezia Reynard. In addition to the poem included in this book, Reynard published at least one poem in a fanzine. We were unable to find any other information about her.

Lilla Price Savino (1881-1939), daughter of poet Lilla Pool Price, published one poem in *Weird Tales* in addition to writing several letters to its letters column, "The Eyrie." We can find no other publications by her.[23]

Edna Bell Seward (1877–1963) published eight stories and poems in adventure, detective, and horror magazines. Her life was like something out of a thriller: her abusive first husband kidnapped their children; and with the help of her sister, Edna staged a daring rescue involving a steamboat, a town under a smallpox quarantine, and a dramatic court case.[24]

Gerald Chan Sieg. See page 72.

Katherine Drayton Mayrant Simons (1890–1969). Poetry may have been Simons's primary genre, but she wrote in every form: novels, nonfiction, short stories, articles, reviews, drama, and even a ballet sketch. She penned three poetry books, the first under the pseudonym "Kadra Maysi," created by taking the first few letters of each of her four names. As Maysi, she wrote three stories for *Weird Tales*. She earned her bachelor's degree from Converse College in South Carolina, where she lived her whole life. In 1952, Converse awarded her an honorary doctorate for her contributions to South Carolina literature.[25]

Grace Stillman. In addition to the poem included in this book, Stillman may have published a poem in *Occult Digest* in 1941, and may be the Grace Stillman Minck who was welcomed to the staff of the *Anacortes* (Washington) *American* in 1936 as "a bride" whose "collection of poems numbers over 600."[26]

Vivian Stratton. In addition to her two poems in *Weird Tales*, Stratton had stories and poems in magazines as diverse as *Street & Smith's Love Story Magazine*, *Radio Craft Magazine*, and *Out West Magazine*.

Katherine van der Veer. In addition to three poems published in *Weird Tales* in 1934 and 1935, van der Veer had work appear in the *Atlantic* and *American Poetry Journal* alongside e.e. cummings and Mark Van Doren. She lived at least part of her life in Yonkers, New York, and published two poetry collections and a guidebook to garden herbs.

Gertrude Wright. We suspect that this was one of the many pseudonyms employed by Lilith Lorraine (see p. 54).

Your Tireless Editors

Jaclyn Youhana Garver's debut novel *Then, Again* came out from Lake Union Publishing in November 2024. She is the author of the poetry chapbook *The Men I Never:*, which was originally published by dancing girl press, and her story "The Butterfly Catcher" appeared in From Beyond Press's *This World Belongs to Us: An Anthology of Horror Stories About Bugs*. She is represented by KT Literary Agency. Jaclyn lives in Fort Wayne, Indiana, with her spouse, Jeff. Follow her on Instagram @JYoGarver.

Michael W. Phillips Jr. is the EIC and publisher of From Beyond Press. He's the editor of *This World Belongs to Us*, *Fettered and Other Tales of Terror* by Greye La Spina, and *This Is Life: Rediscovered Short Fiction* by Frank London Brown, and the co-editor (with Jennifer Jeanne McArdle) of *Escalators to Hell: Shopping Mall Horrors*. He's the co-author (with Rebecca Zorach) of *Gold: Nature and Culture* (Reaktion Books). His work has appeared in *Disturbed Digest* and *Grievous Angel* and is forthcoming from the *Magazine of Fantasy & Science Fiction*.

Notes

Our main sources for biographical information, aside from specific items noted here, were Wikipedia and Terence E. Hanley's Tellers of Weird Tales (ToWT) blog, tellersofweirdtales.blogspot.com

1. Texas Jewish Historical Society, "From Our Archives: Rita Barr," 2024.
2. *Rapid City Journal* 8/29/2000.
3. *Boston Globe* 12/12/1954.
4. *San Bernardino County* Sun 5/21/1938.
5. ToWT.
6. *Somerset Daily American* 5/21/1975.
7. Various articles in the *Kansas City Star*, 1940s and 1950s.
8. ToWT, Wikipedia.
9. ToWT.
10. ToWT, Wikipedia.
11. *New York Times* 7/15/1987; Alabama Yesterdays blog 4/9/2021.
12. Wikipedia.
13. ToWT.
14. ToWT.
15. *Detroit Free Press* 2/2/1975.
16. ToWT.
17. ToWT.
18. ToWT.
19. Archives West, archiveswest.orbiscascade.org/ark:80444/xv35229
20. ToWT.
21. Wikipedia.
22. ToWT.
23. ToWT.
24. ToWT.
25. ToWT; South Carolina Encyclopedia.
26. *Anacortes American* 6/11/1936; *Occult Digest* November 1941.